HOBO AND ME

HOBO AND ME

A novel by

Elizabeth Fritz

HOBO AND ME

iUniverse books may be ordered through booksellers or by contacting:

*iUniverse
1663 Liberty Drive
Bloomington, IN 47403
www.iuniverse.com
1-800-Authors (1-800-288-4677)*

ISBN: 978-1-4917-4612-7 (sc)

Printed in the United States of America.

iUniverse rev. date: 09/29/2014

ALSO BY ELIZABETH FRITZ

Surprise Surprise
Cousin Delia's Legacy
Hope's Journey
Trio
Assisted Living—Or Dying
Athena
Hunting Giovane
Prosperity
Magnolias and Murder
Clio

The author gratefully acknowledges the contributions of front cover photographer, Jean Moore-Palm and of Kende Hare whose Mohanna graciously posed as Hobo for the photo.

The letter arrived on Friday, April 1. The envelope lay in glaring contrast to the routine riff-raff of bills and trashy fliers that had accompanied it into my mail box. I turned it over in my hands twice to savor the heft of its fine paper and quality of its inscriptions. The return address was especially elegant.

Bocce, O'Leary, and Shapiro
Attorneys at Law
One Monroe Plaza
Columbia, Indiana

For a moment I imagined Archie Bunker's favorable reaction to a legal firm of such ethnic diversity. Although typed in impeccable pica on an IBM Selectric with a carbon ribbon, my address seemed positively plebeian:

Miss Rebecca Jane Bell
Apartment 5B, 3445 Douglas Street
Shady Grove, Indiana

I was so impressed that I dispensed with my usual rough-and-ready rip-and-tear treatment of envelopes; I got a steak knife from the kitchen drawer and slit the flap neatly. The single sheet inside lived up to grandeur of the envelope. A handsome letterhead was flanked in the right corner by three numbers: local phone, toll-free, and FAX. On the left, a column headed *Associates* displayed twelve names complete with their LLBs and JDs. The body of the letter was brief and to the point.

Miss Bell,

I write as the executor of the estate of your late kinsman, William George Bell, to inform you that a substantial legacy awaits you. Please contact me at your earliest convenience by telephone, FAX, or letter to arrange a meeting.

Very truly yours,

Daniel X. O'Leary, Esquire

The first surprise for me was the word "kinsman." Fatherless at birth, motherless at age 5, and deprived of foster parents by an auto accident at 19—as far as I knew my kinship was a blank. I had never heard of William George Bell although I was prepared to enjoy any kinship linked to the words of the second surprise, "substantial legacy." I was without a job. Rent and credit card and car payments loomed in my immediate future, to say nothing of soaring gas and grocery prices. It crossed my mind that this might be a cruel hoax although I doubted a scammer would invest in such classy stationery. I glanced up at the clock, 5:15, and grabbed the phone to dial the 800 number. A disembodied voice answered on the first ring.

"The offices of Bocce, O'Leary, and Shapiro are closed until 9 A.M. Monday." CLICK.

Disappointed though not surprised, I hit REDIAL just to make sure and got the same result.

"I'll be back on Monday at 9 A.M." I told the robot. "Bet on it!"

In the meantime, I set out to rummage the documentary evidence of my existence. From the footlocker stowed in my closet, I took a scuffed brown leather portfolio. Spreading its contents on the kitchen table, I began arranging them in a rough chronology. First, my birth certificate recording: Mother <u>Louise May Bell</u>, Father <u>a blank line</u>, live birth of a <u>female child</u>, birth date <u>September 4, 1981</u>. A red-white-and-blue card announcing my Social Security number. A yellowed newspaper clipping, headline FOUR DEAD IN FIRE AT HUDSON ELECTRONICS, text listing names, Louise Bell among them, survived by one child. A copy of a court order placing Rebecca Jane Bell in foster care with Douglas and Mary Conrad. Then there was a bunch of stuff that Mary Conrad had saved from school days: records of immunizations, grade cards, even a note from my fourth grade teacher. "Rebecca has been chosen Flower Princess for our play. She will need a costume, a simple full-length sleeveless dress, white with a yellow ribbon sash and a crown of artificial daisies. The Craft Barn has the materials for you at a very reasonable price." There was also a black-and-white photo of the princess, skinny, gawky, the flower crown perched at a dangerous angle on a head of long, straggly hair. Mary had saved every certificate of every achievement, tied them up in a bundle with a red ribbon, and topped the bundle with my high school diploma. A memento of the Conrads' funeral, a simple card with a Bible verse, brought mist to my eyes. Uncle Doug and Aunt Mary had been very good to me. Mother's insurance and their supplements had given me a start on my college education; scholarships and my many part time jobs had finished it up.

On my own I had included subsequent records in the portfolio: my diploma, BA with honors in language arts from Indiana University; the grants and fellowships that sent me to France for two years to polish my French and German skills; my passport visaed for a dozen European countries. Shuffled among those items was a gaudy postcard depicting the Eiffel Tower. Idly I turned it over and discovered it addressed to Lou and Becca Bell with the message "Isn't this something? Hope you can see it sometime for yourselves" and signed "Cousin Willy G." Willy G! That triggered hazy memories of stories my mother had told me long ago. In those days the adventures of Cousin Willy G and his dog Hobo ranked right up there with Dr. Seuss books. Was Cousin Willy G the kinsman, William George Bell, whose "substantial legacy" Daniel O'Leary had for me? Maybe!

After restoring the documents to the portfolio, I decided to walk downtown for something to eat. I chose the Villa Romana and began a weekend of pondering what the words *substantial legacy* might mean. Over the Villa's menu, I vacillated between pizza with a mug of beer ($6.99) and fettucini Alfredo with Caesar salad and glass of house red ($14.99). Was *substantial* sufficiently promising to justify a major expenditure? But leery of counting chickens before they hatched, I settled on the lesser cost that left my mouth watering for the greater one. On Saturday morning, I bundled up my stuff for the Laundromat and while watching the whirling riot behind the drier window, weighed the desirability of a new outfit to adorn myself for the proposed meeting with O'Leary. Did I dare to risk $65 or $75 on the sale racks of The Vogue? I decided it wouldn't hurt to look. Maybe hearing the exact amount of a *substantial legacy* was worth a stylish addition to my shabby wardrobe. On the way home I stopped at the bookstore and lingered over a featured $27.00 hard copy novel on the *New York Times* bestseller list. Regretfully I settled on a $2.99 paperback thriller languishing on the remainder table. A cheap read might take my mind off the promised legacy. Sunday morning in church, I dropped a fiver in the collection plate in lieu of my usual single. I felt guilty about bribing God to assure that my *substantial legacy* would be a sizable reimbursement but I apologized to Him in my bedtime prayer.

Monday 9 A.M. finally came and on the dot I dialed the toll-free number. Instead of the robot I heard the lilt of a cheerful soprano: "Offices of Bocce, O'Leary, and Shapiro. This is Jennifer. How may I help you?"

I stammered what I knew was more than what she wanted to hear of my business. Her response was another verse of the song: "I'll put you through to our Miss Bain. She does our scheduling. Hold, please. It will only be a moment."

Miss Bain's voice was not melodious, it was instead crisp and businesslike, no words wasted: "Miss Bell, we expected your call. How would this Wednesday at 1 P.M. suit you? Do you have pencil and paper to take down directions to our offices?"

In less than 45 seconds, I was scheduled and dismissed: "Thank you for calling." CLICK. Just to make sure that I was doing the right thing, I called the Better Business Bureau and asked if Bocce, O'Leary, and Shapiro was a reputable firm. The woman who took my call couldn't have been more outraged had I questioned the Immaculate Conception. "Certainly!" she said. "Best in this part of the state!"

My morning's telephone encounters encouraged a visit to The Vogue, where I purchased a tweedy blazer in green and rust, an off-white shell, and brown slacks. Not only might a nicely coordinated ensemble play well with Mr. O'Leary, but it would be essential for interviews I hoped for when I signed up with the unemployment office this week. In January the legislature had publicized a goal of drastic cuts in the state budget; education funding was hit particularly hard. Consequently every school system in the state had scurried to slash its budget for the coming year. In February I had been informed that my current teaching contract with the Shady Grove School System would lapse as of March 1. French and German were being dropped from the curriculum. I had frantically bombarded every high school and college in the state with résumés and requests for employment applications. Only seven had even bothered to reply; each of their letters began with "Due to the legislature's cuts in funding and in view of the current economic climate…." News like that had sent me to the library every afternoon to pore over help wanted ads in the classified sections of in-state newspapers. The contacts I pursued promptly taught me I was overqualified for McJobs and underqualified for anything else; pessimism made the words *substantial legacy* glimmer like a pot of gold at the foot of an optimistic rainbow. Even if the legacy was fool's gold, I prepared myself to go out and fight the "current economic climate" for a place in the sun.

I came home and tried on my new clothes, drawing encouragement from their trim fit and becoming colors. My last hairdo, cleverly cut in a smooth cap and its soft brown shade discreetly colored with gold highlights, still looked good. The mirror told me that *I* looked good: nice clear complexion, bright brown eyes, firm chin, and straight teeth (thanks to Doug Conrad who had given up smoking to pay for orthodontia). I dragged out my brown loafers and remedied the scuffs with a vigorous application of dark brown Crayola. Flat-heeled shoes were always critical to the overall impression I hoped to convey to male interviewers. I prayed that O'Leary was NOT short, balding, and overweight. Men like that tended to be intimidated by a female beanpole six feet one inch tall. I, however, had resigned myself at age 16 that there was no way to make myself shorter and had compensated by practicing erect posture, squared shoulders, and thinking bedamned to them as found me ungainly. That peace of mind, once achieved, allowed me to forget about my height, except when considering shoe styles and quality.

Arriving at the palatial offices of Bocce, O'Leary, and Shapiro, I identified myself. The dulcet-voiced Tiffany stationed at the reception desk presided over a multi-buttoned console that looked more appropriate to the cockpit of a Boeing 707 than to a law office. I waited a few minutes for her to master the array of buttons and flashing red lights and to announce my arrival. Finally a diminutive white-haired woman appeared, invited me to be seated in the anteroom of O'Leary's office, and offered me coffee, tea, soda, or lemonade. I declined any. I've never understood why liquid refreshment is supposed to pacify a person kept waiting for an appointment. If one is already nervous, fluid just stimulates a visit to the rest room. I had foreseen this ploy; the rest room in the lobby had met my needs before I sought out my business destination.

A surreptitious glance at my watch showed 1:40 before the elderly woman, responding to a flashing light at her desk, showed me into the inner sanctum. O'Leary rose to greet me and advanced with outstretched hand. Blessedly, he was a full head taller than I, white-haired, in the 60s but youthful in looks and mien. Bright blue eyes, a pleasant smile on his ruggedly handsome face, and his agreeable voice immediately won my confidence.

"Sorry to keep you waiting—a long distance call from a garrulous client. I've been looking forward to this meeting. Mr. Bell could tell me very little about you. He said he had never seen you although he and your mother had corresponded intermittently before her death."

"The only correspondence that survived is a postcard from Cousin Willy G. I've been wondering if Cousin Willy was the kinsman your letter referred to."

"Yes, Mr. Bell told me he was your mother's second cousin once removed and that the family called him Willy G to distinguish him from another cousin, William Bernard, Willy B, that is. He lost track of you after the tragedy of your mother's death. In fact, he had to hire a detective to find you when he decided to make you his heir. He intended to get in touch with you personally but his death intervened. He was 97. I should fill in some facts before discussing the terms of his legacy." The lawyer cleared his throat before continuing.

"Mr. Bell was eccentric, a brilliant inventor, a multimillionaire due to his inventions, and very proud of his lineage. He put the bulk of his wealth into a trust but was determined to keep two things alive after his death: Bald Knob and Hobo. Bald Knob is the Bell homestead on 1600 or so acres, semi-mountainous, almost all forested, non-arable, located in southern Indiana. Hobo is his beloved dog, a 2-year old German Shepherd, or Alsatian as some would say. Mr. Bell's testamentary arrangements reflect his passionate attachment to Bald Knob and Hobo. You will undoubtedly find them very unconventional."

"In what way? I'm finding his very existence unconventional, since I never heard of him except as a mythical character whose adventures with a dog named Hobo were the stuff of bedtime stories told me by my mother. I can't even imagine why he would want to leave me a legacy."

"Let me explain his wealth first. As an inventor, he had hundreds of patents, most of them quite profitably licensed for the long term. He knew of no kin other than yourself and did not want his wealth to revert to the state or to charities in which he had no interest, hence the Bell Trust. He came to me with two goals: one to preserve the Bell homestead where he was born and died; the other to provide for Hobo...."

"Hobo? That dog must be long dead."

"One of Mr. Bell's little quirks is that he had had one dog after another during his lifetime, each named Hobo. I won't read Mr. Bell's will to you. It's very long and complicated, consisting as it does of an inventory of his inventions, patents, and investments. Instead I'll cut to the chase. You are to have it all providing that you contract with the Bell Trust to make the Bell homestead your primary domicile and make a home for Hobo until the end of his natural life."

I was stunned. "What? That's crazy! Why didn't he just leave it all to the dog and designate someone as guardian for him. I don't know how to deal with huge wealth or how to look after an old house or a dog. I don't even *want* a lot of money. I haven't told you but I am out of a job at the moment, due to the cuts to education in the current state budget. When I read your letter, I was only hoping for a little money to keep me afloat until I found a job."

"Let me explain the details of the contract. If you agree to a contract with the Trust, it will pay you a monthly salary of $10,000 as long as Hobo lives and you live on the Bell homestead. Take note that is $120,000 a year. I would expect you could live very comfortably on that."

I gasped in disbelief, but O'Leary continued, "The Trust will also pay all expenses for maintaining the house, lands, and Hobo, as well as staff should you decide you want household help. The contract will require you to live in the homestead at least eight months of the year; otherwise you will be free to live anywhere you like. It will, however, require you to keep and care for Hobo wherever you live. Although the old Bell homestead is not a palace, it has every modern amenity and comfort. Think about it. It's not a bad deal, especially since the whole of the trust will revert to you upon Hobo's death."

I sat agape. "I'm stunned. I don't know what to think. I can't believe that anyone would conjure up a deal like this one. An annual salary of $120,000 is more than an ordinary schoolteacher can aspire to! Furthermore, what kind of a dog is Hobo? How long is he likely to live? How do I know we could get along with one another?"

"Hobo is an Alsatian, in common parlance a German shepherd. He is presently two years old and his breed has an average lifespan of twelve to fifteen years. Mr. Bell has trained him to obey every command for appropriate living both indoors and out. Mr. Bell described his temperament as 'sweet.' I have met the dog only once but on that occasion, he was friendly and perfectly behaved although reserved."

"I don't know…." I drew a long breath, "I'm flummoxed by all of this."

"Why don't you pay a visit to the Bell homestead? Look it over and meet the dog? I can give you 30 days to make up your mind about signing the contract."

"What if I choose not to sign the contract?"

"The trust would revert to various charities named by Mr. Bell. Hobo would be sent to a shelter, hopefully to be adopted."

"The storybook Hobo was a beloved friend in my childhood. A shelter sounds pretty heartless." Grudgingly I said, "I'll look things over and let you know within thirty days if I will or won't."

"Fine. Do you need any money to tide you over? I can advance you few hundred dollars."

I admitted that an advance would be helpful and his little white-haired secretary wrote out a check for $500, and provided me with directions to the Bell homestead. We parted with a handshake. I sat in the car fingering the check for an hour before I started to return to Shady Grove. Few of the many notions running through my head wore dollar signs.

On Friday morning, I was in the hill country of southern Indiana, heading for Corona, the small town nearest the Bell homestead. I was threading narrow, winding roads, some perched on the shoulders of impressive limestone outthrusts not quite deserving to be called mountains but certainly more massy and rugged than hills. The road to Corona followed a stream purling over a rocky bed in a valley lined with oak and poplar saplings and underbrush among a scanty growth of mature trees. As a city girl, I could not identify little trees flowering in clouds of pink or white flowers on branches just beginning to burst into foliage. All I could do was admire their beauty. Obviously flora in these parts had to work hard to stay upright; roots probed the stony outcrops like fingers clutching Mother Earth for dear life. Now and then rounding a loop, the road looked over a pocket of weedy meadow where the ruins of a shanty testified to failed hopes for agriculture.

Corona announced itself with a bullet-pocked sign and the information "Pop. 453" although once I was in its main street, I suspected the count was grossly overstated. A general store-cum-gas station stood on one corner of a cross-street, a small brick church on another. A hardware store, its windows vacant and dusty, crumbled on the third corner, and on the fourth a tiny shack in the middle of a huge parking lot sported a barber pole. A few unpretentious houses clad in vinyl siding stood under mammoth oaks on graveled streets leading from the main drag.

I stopped at the general store for directions to the Bell homestead. I found the storekeeper lounging in a decrepit recliner, a *People* magazine draped open over his face. When my entry set the bell on the door a-jangle, he roused to heave himself out of the chair. He was short, fat, and elderly with a beard big enough and wild enough for submission to the Guinness Book; his stance was truculent and his greeting curt.

"Hey! The quarry is on down the road but there's no one there today."

"I'm not looking for a quarry. I'm looking for…."

"Sorry for the mistake. People who come in here are usually looking for the quarry, but they're hardly ever women. I guess I should be grateful for the change. What can I do for you?"

"I'm hoping you can direct me to William Bell's house."

"He's dead, six weeks now. Whaddaya want at Bald Knob?"

I decided this was an encounter with either local prejudice to strangers or protection of an old-time resident's privacy. So the best thing to do was to level with him.

"My name is Rebecca Bell. William Bell was a relative who left me an interest in his house. His lawyers suggested that I should come to look it over."

"If you're thinkin' of buyin,' I can tell you it's no place for weekend hangout for a good-lookin' city woman. Willy was pretty much a hermit up there on Bald Knob, only neighbor is a crazy old woman who makes pots and she ain't all that close by. You wouldn't like Bald Knob nor her. 'Sides she don't sell her pots to drop-ins."

I decided to overlook his belligerence and persevere in my inquiry. He finally came around and grudgingly pointed me to the upslope of the cross-street. A sign said Hudson Road.

"Can't miss it, got a red mail box on the left side of the road. The road ain't too good but there's not likely any traffic. My name's Burr Worman and I'm on the phone. I deliver when the weather lets me."

The road was definitely *not too good*, in fact it was just plain scary, bare rock and sparsely graveled dirt, very narrow, crowded on the left side by sheer cliffs and on the right by either thick undergrowth or sharp dropoffs. I drove it, with teeth clenched and breath often suspended. The red mailbox was a welcome sight. It was perched atop an enormous pottery replica of a bell, perhaps a neighborly gesture of the crazy old woman potter.

I turned in and started on a steep-sloping twisting lane, fairly wide and walled by large jagged boulders. The lane led me to the top of the mini-alp that gave the place its name, a bald knob ringed with evergreens. On the very top of the eminence there stood a sprawling two-story building, part log and part clapboard. Four large stone chimneys anchored it to the site. In contrast to the prevailing architectural style in this part of the state, there was no sign of dilapidation. The windows sparkled, the veranda facing the approach was well swept, evergreen shrubbery softened the rough outlines of the foundation, dark red shingles covered a gabled roof. The drive continued around the house to a wide parking area in the back where a red barn stood on a somewhat lower elevation. A man worked on a tractor in the open barn door. A large black and tan dog stood on the alert beside him.

I parked and waited. The man and the dog came toward the car. The man was very tall, burly and muscular, not yet middle-aged. When he doffed his baseball cap in greeting, I saw he was blond, blue-eyed, quite good looking, and already had a sunburn. I put the window down to speak to him but he forestalled me.

"You must be Miss Rebecca. Mr. O'Leary told me to expect you sometime this week. I'm Andreas van Houten, my spread is just over the ridge. I helped Mr. Willy during his last days and have kept the place going since he passed. Don't let Hobo scare you. He's standoffish with strangers but never aggressive unless commanded or provoked."

"Glad to meet you. Will Hobo mind if I get out of the car?"

"'Course not, but I hope you are wearing sensible shoes. The gravel on this lot is tricky for ladies with high heels."

"Not to worry. I came prepared for guided tours over rough terrain." Slowly I betook myself from the car, one eye on Hobo and one on the footing. Standing to shake hands with van Houten I noticed at once that he topped me by a good six inches, even in my jogging shoes. "If you talked to Mr. O'Leary, you must know why I've come. I couldn't consider the possibility of living here and looking after Hobo without getting a feel for the house and a relationship with the dog. I'll be honest, I have more qualms about meeting Hobo than about living in this remote location. Two years of hosteling in Europe taught me how to live in country without conveniences. But I don't know anything about dogs, never had one or been around one."

He grinned. "Let's start with the house. You'll be surprised by its conveniences."

This side (back?) of the house featured another veranda, this one furnished with four white-painted rocking chairs. At the door van Houten pulled a bunch of keys from his pocket.

"When Mr. Willy began to weaken, he gave me keys for everything because I came every day to check on him. I found him…." Van Houten's voice faded to an emotional rasp as he turned the key in the lock. I suspected a warm friendship with Cousin Willy and lasting sorrow for his death.

The door swung open and van Houten stepped back to let Hobo enter first. We followed into a very large room with a floor of broad planks made smooth and white by many years of vigorous scrubbing. The room was empty except for a cluster of leather sofas and chairs around the fireplace at one end. A closed door on the wall opposite to the fireplace seemed to access the clapboard section of the building. The layout of this house immediately confused me. I had taken the front of the building to be what I first saw as I drove up the lane, but the interior seemed to favor the side facing the barn as its front. A wide hall led directly from this large room to another exterior door and another veranda on the front (or back, I couldn't say). The left hand side of this hall was a blank wall but several doors stood open on its right hand side. As van Houten allowed me to stand for a moment to survey the arrangement, Hobo made a cursory reconnoiter into every room with an open door.

"What's he doing, Mr. van Houten? Looking for his master?"

"Call me Andy like Mr. Willy did. No need for formality. Mr. Willy trained Hobo to scout the house for intruders. Until I signed up with him, the house often stood empty for weeks while Mr. Willy and Hobo were on the road attending to Mr. Willy's affairs."

Pointing to the closed door in the wall opposite the fireplace, Andy began to explain a complicated layout.

"This door goes to the part of the house that Mr. Willy built on in the 40s after he inherited it. It's two-story, clapboard on the outside. He had a basement dug out beneath it to hold the services for the whole house: A/C, furnace, electrical panels, water softener, and such. It used to have a boiler that served radiators but Mr. Willy removed them a few years ago and put in multi-zoned electric baseboard heating; he also made the hot water system tankless. It can get very cold up here on the knob sometimes, so there's still a gas furnace and forced air for backup; the furnace and point-of-use water heating is fueled by a big propane tank in the barn. The indoor temperature of the whole house stays at 75 degrees year-round. The propane tank is filled twice a year, standing order. The house and barn are on Ohio Power and Light, but the generator in the barn kicks in if there's an interruption. The water supply is a 400-foot well and water quality is excellent."

"Whew!" My only comment expressed my amazement. "Here we are in the middle of nowhere, and Cousin Willy was born in this log house almost 100 years ago! Where did he get his ideas for space age living?"

"TV kept him abreast of change and he traveled regularly to trade shows all over the world. He was an inventor and rich enough to indulge his every whim. On the right hand side of this hall, the log house is still here, conventionally furnished and updated in every aspect, still treasured. The second floor of the log house has been extended over the clapboard section in order to provide more bedrooms. There's more space age stuff in the kitchen. Wait till you see!"

Turning, Andy led me away from the big room, flipping light switches as he went. The rooms on the right hand side of the hall were furnished with stylish chairs, tables, and lamps set on handsome area rugs spread on the plank floors. One room was definitely a well-stocked library, bookshelves floor to ceiling, divans and lighting designed for comfortable reading. A quick glimpse showed me recent titles stacked on side tables. Another huge fireplace completed the library.

Hobo had tagged along in the hall but here he entered to spend time thoroughly sniffing the cushions of every divan. Andy volunteered an explanation.

"Hobo and Mr. Willy spent a lot of time in the library in recent years. Hobo still looks for him every time we come in here."

To me the library was so far the most attractive feature of the offer of O'Leary's contract. I could imagine hours spent there, book in hand, feet on an ottoman, a fire glowing on the hearth. Flowering foliage depicted in stained glass glimmered in windows bracketing the chimney. Hobo sprawled … where? I knew he would be close wherever Cousin Willy might be.

Andy seemed to read my mind. "Hobo was usually on the sofa beside Mr. Willy with his head on his leg." He chuckled, "Sometimes I caught both of them snoring."

Another room appeared to be an office. I gave it only a glance. I would reserve closer scrutiny to a later time. The kitchen, however, was a shock. I stood still in silent awe: a vaulted ceiling with skylights, countertops in cool gray granite, floors of gray ceramic tile mottled with faint pink highlights, all appliances stainless steel, cabinetry cherry wood, the layout designed for maximum efficiency. I could imagine the lyrical tones of a realtor if ever one was commissioned to sell this house. The kitchen occupied the fireplace end of a room that stretched the full width of the log house. Plank floors survived in the other end of the space which was done up as an "eat-in" area. Although an ambitious realtor would studiously avoid mentioning the absence of a formal dining room, he or she would be quick to emphasize the hutch with glass shelves decked with bright tableware, a glass-topped table, and six chairs of polished steel, cushioned in red vinyl. Tall, broad windows showcased a view of the wooded down-slope of the knob, a view of small trees covered in this season by clouds of pink or white flowers. When I commented on the color, Andy said it was dogwood and wild plum in the spring, red maple and golden aspen leaves in the fall.

Now Hobo was following us, unobtrusively but very assiduously. To cover up my nervousness over his silent attention I resorted to a trivial observation. I confessed to Andy that I was stumped. Was I to call the kitchen door leading to the veranda, and more rocking chairs, the *front* door? Or the *back* door? He laughed and said "Call it whatever. Mr. Willy called it the *other* door most of the time. Say, did you come prepared to stay the night?"

"I have an overnight case in the car, but maybe there's not a bedroom available here and I'd better find a motel nearby."

"Let's go upstairs. There are plenty of beds. The cleaners were here two weeks ago to dust and vacuum the whole house. The linen closets are full of clean bedclothes if you wouldn't mind making up a bed."

Doors at the junction of the log and clapboard sections of the house opened on a pair of stairs, one down, one up. On the second floor the downstairs hall was repeated but here doors on both sides led to bedroom suites, each nicely decorated in attractive colors. The gabled roof of the building afforded a beautiful bathroom and a walk-in closet for each bedroom. Two of the bathrooms had both a spa tub and a capacious shower stall. All boasted granite counters and splash-backs on vanities fitted with twin vessel-sinks and ceramic tile on the floors and around the tubs. A linen closet completed each bath room.

I shook my head in disbelief. "Did Cousin Willy design these rooms? Why so many bedrooms and such elegance?"

"He surely did do things his way. He always said he had no one to please but himself. As for all the suites, he said 'in the old days' he entertained a lot, clients for his inventions, friends he met in his travels. He joked that once he hit his 80th year, he thought up bedroom suites for pastime, thinking he might want some day to run a bed and breakfast. Twelve years ago he and I met at a trade fair in Amsterdam and enjoyed our friendship so much that he talked me into emigrating to the U.S. He put me up in one of these suites while I was looking for land to buy, but as far as I know I was his only guest then or since. This corner bedroom with the view of the dogwood was his. Let's go back down and I'll show you the rest of the downstairs."

Hobo rejoined us at the bottom of the stair. Apparently he didn't care for or wasn't welcomed on the second floor. Andy indicated a door down opposite the stair up and said it led to the basement for laundry, a wine cellar, and other services. Then he and I returned to the big room where we had first entered. Andy approached the plain paneled door in the wall facing the fireplace. When he turned the knob and the door swung open, a second door appeared. Solid steel or steel-clad, I couldn't tell which, but it took another of Andy's keys to operate the lever that opened it. Inside there seemed to be two rooms, one behind the other. The first room was devoted to file cabinets, except for one corner where a formidable gray steel door loomed, obviously thick, and fitted with levers and a wheel with a combination dial in its hub.

"That looks like a bank vault!" I gasped.

Andy laughed. "Next thing to it. That's one thing I've never had a key for. It sits on a concrete base rising from the basement floor and the chamber is sheathed with four inches of reinforced concrete. I've been wondering if anyone other than Mr. Willy knew the combination."

"What's in it? Money? Valuables?"

"I can answer that, sort of. Mr. Willy told me it held the drawings for his most valuable inventions and only he and Hobo knew the combination. You'll have to ask Mr. O'Leary if Mr. Willy left any word with him."

"How could Hobo know the combination?"

"You'll have to ask him."

Hobo had taken up a post in front of the vault door and now sat stubbornly silent, in no way welcoming an inquiry. The file cabinets wore labels identifying their respective contents; none were locked. The only lighting in this room was an overhead bank of fluorescent bulbs. The door into the second room was not locked. After we entered, Hobo followed and planted himself in the opening. His stance telegraphed a message to anyone else venturing in: *On guard! No entry!* The room contained two drafting tables, a couple of stools, and several tables. One table had a partially-assembled gadget posed on its metal top and was on wheels to facilitate rotation in any direction. Loose parts, a sketch book, and a pencil lay beside the gadget. "A work in progress," I whispered reverently.

Other tables held an orderly array of miniature machines. "Are these toys?" I asked.

"No," Andy replied. "Mr. Willy used them for making his models." He opened the wall cupboards and pointed out tiny, exquisite mechanisms lined up on the shelves. This room was brightly lit throughout by lamps on metal-clad extensions like goose neck fixtures dangling from the ceiling. Looking around the room, I saw the single window was barred by multiple layers of steel mesh. If one had been able to see out of it, the view would be of the drive that wound around the house to the rear parking area. I had not noticed anything odd about it when I drove by. Later I learned that from the outside, the window was a mirror, its muttins mimicking those of the real windows of the house. As we left the area Andy locked it up again.

I had made up my mind as we came down from the upstairs sleeping quarters that I would be staying overnight. The house seemed to present a mystery veiled in a shroud that was both remarkable and unremarkable, an indescribably super-modern shell housing a quirky old man's unfathomable whims. I was beginning to wish I had known Cousin Willy. His quirks were the marks of a genius.

"Andy, I think I'll stay tonight. Is there anything I should know about the workings of the house."

"No, everything works just as you would expect in any modern house. There's no landline telephone but Mr. Willy had a cell. Do you?"

When I confessed rather sheepishly, no, Andy dug through a drawer in the kitchen and found Cousin Willy's cell and charger and plugged it in. "The number one key calls my phone which I leave on all the time. You'll be wanting some breakfast tomorrow morning. I know for certain there's bread, butter, and orange juice in the kitchen freezer. I don't know what else."

"Great, then all I need is my suitcase from the car."

Within the next 15 minutes, I was in and ready to settle. Andy bade me good-bye, invited me to call if I needed anything, and left Hobo and me alone in the house. Hobo sat calmly, his dark gaze firmly fastened on me, intensifying my nervousness. Cautiously I put one foot ahead of the other and careful to make no sudden moves, promenaded to the kitchen. Hobo padded quietly at my heels. I opened the freezer compartment of the refrigerator and took out the loaf of bread, box of butter, and can of orange juice concentrate that I found there. Arranging them neatly by the sink, I realized I was provided with food but I panicked when I remembered Hobo. But ego kept me from calling Andy to learn how to feed him. I started opening drawers and cupboards and found a door to a pantry with shelves loaded with canned goods. A 50-lb bag of dry dog food leaned against one wall, a stainless steel bowl beside it. Hobo's dinner seemed assured. As I filled the bowl with kibble, I recalled a weeklong assignment to look after a vacationing neighbor's cat and her emphatic instruction. "Don't forget the water! Eating dry food, water must be available all the time!" I saw no water dish so I took down a large serving bowl from the cupboard and filled it from the tap. Hobo watched my flurry to set down food and water from his vantage point just inside the kitchen door, then rose majestically and paced to inspect them. After an approving mouthful of kibble and a slurp of water, he returned to his watch. More panic on my part! He didn't trust my catering! Maybe something else Cousin Willy had trained him for: Never eat what a stranger offers! Then common sense kicked in. Hobo would surely eat when he was hungry. I might be a stranger but we were after all still in his house and he had familiar vittles in front of him.

I gathered my composure and went upstairs to unpack my suitcase and make up the bed in the corner room that Cousin Willy was wont to use. The linen closet was fully stocked: sheets, pillowcases, light blankets, a plump satin duvet, and lavender-scented soap, hand lotion, and toiletries. With the bed made and my pajamas laid out, I ventured downstairs. Hobo was waiting and watching at the foot of the stairs. He followed me to the kitchen where I rejoiced to see the food dish licked clean. I hoped that he and I had crossed one bridge on the road to relationship.

I took off on a perfunctory exploration of the first floor rooms, Hobo tailing me at a discreet distance. He made me feel as if I were under surveillance. Perhaps he expected to be called to testify to pilfering in case any of the silver went missing. I took particular interest in one room done up as an office: big desk, ergonomic desk chair, laptop computer on the desk, a printer and a scanner on a credenza, stationery supplies neatly stowed in cabinets. A 65-inch plasma TV hung on a wall opposite a plump leather recliner; a pamphlet on the desk listed 250 available satellite stations. I sat down in that impressive desk chair and Hobo tucked himself under the desk by my feet. I began to feel at home and the immediate presence of the dog was oddly welcoming.

I was struck with the thought that maybe, just maybe, I could make a dream come true. I had always wanted to do a modern translation of *Les Miserables* but always had balked at the drudgery of handwriting and polishing a manuscript. A little experience at Shady Grove High School had introduced me to the advantages of word processing. I imagined myself at this desk, tickling the keyboard of this computer, working on my dream. Perhaps I could have Cousin Willy's work cleared off the hard disk under Mr. O'Leary's supervision…. But remembering a whole flock of unhatched chickens, I backed off from those notions. I had not decided to sign that crazy contract. Was I going to? Or was I just letting myself be tempted? My castles in Spain evaporated as a major pang of hunger made itself known. I remembered seeing a can of tuna fish in the pantry. If I could find a can opener....

I was successful in making a tuna fish sandwich, had even found an unopened jar of mayonnaise for lubrication. The orange juice had thawed and I reconstituted it. My sandwich and the juice made quite a satisfactory supper. As I sat eating it at the glass-topped table, Hobo walked up to me, uttered one peremptory bark, and sat down, pinning his gaze on my face. He wanted something! What, I wondered. He had food, and water, what was left? Of course, he wanted to go out! I opened the door to the front (other?) veranda and he scampered off. In just a few minutes, he was back at the door and another peremptory bark informed me he wanted in! We had achieved two-way communication. A second bridge to relationship! Or so I hoped.

Next, like a magnet, that library drew me. I looked at and caressed book after book: a whole set of Kipling novels and short stories; another complete set of Dickens, including *Edwin Drood* and *Dombey and Son*, neither of which I had ever read; a tattered copy of *Moby Dick*, a favorite of mine as well; an assortment of recent books by respected pundits; a host of biographies of American and English notables; a lot of history, covering ancient to modern times, every book showing evidence of having been read and often reread. I puttered around the shelves until I noticed that nightfall had drained the color from the stained glass panes. Time for bed, and suddenly I was very tired. I had risen at 5 A.M. to get an early start for the Bell homestead.

A glass of water for a nightcap, refills on Hobo's food and water dishes, and responses to his signals at the door—and I was ready to go up to bed. I found everything needful for a relaxing shower and luxuriated in high-end bathroom linens, the like of which I had never been able to afford. Once my hair was dry, teeth brushed, and pajamas donned, I was ready to slip into bed. I was struggling with the latch on the casement windows when I heard Hobo's nails clattering on the stairs and bedroom floor. I turned to see him diving under the bed and emerging with a large oval rug firmly gripped in his teeth. Bracing his feet, he hauled the rug into position across the bedroom door, took three turns on it, collapsed into a ball, and laid his head on his forepaws. The second floor, taboo in the daytime, seemed to become a guard post when the master bed was occupied. Obviously the dog was accustomed to sleeping at night within call of Cousin Willy. For me, unfamiliar country noises were a bit daunting, and it was reassuring to know that Hobo was favoring me with his company. I slept like a log.

I woke to blinding sunlight pouring in the open window. Hobo had deserted his rug. I bounded out of bed and hastily smoothed the covers. The room was chilly; I closed the window and the room immediately grew warmer. A few quick licks, my morning grooming was complete, and I was down the stairs and opening the door where Hobo stood ready for his morning constitutional. Upon his return he immediately sat down at his empty food dish and looked at me with what I interpreted as anticipation. I wondered if I was starting to get the hang of canine communication. Once the food dish was empty, Hobo posted himself at the door to the hall to begin his version of morning grooming, noisily licking his face, forepaws, and private parts.

I organized my supply of bread, butter, and orange juice, and rummaged the pantry to find a box of tea bags, an unopened jar of strawberry jam, and a canister of sugar. After I found a tea kettle in one of the cupboards and put water on to boil, I sat down to quite a satisfying breakfast. I was enjoying my hot beverage when I nearly jumped out of my skin. A voice! The walls were talking!

"Good morning! Andy here. May I come in?"

Hobo was unmoved but my screech echoed shock when I talked back to empty air. "Where are you? You've scared me out of my skin. Of course, you can come in. You have a key."

"I'm in. You've been introduced to the voice-activated intercom. You didn't lock the door last night. I'm not scolding but you will have to make locking up a habit." Now the voice was in the hall and Hobo rose lazily to greet it.

Andy was dressed in a bright red mackinaw, a woolly cap, jeans, and heavy boots. His cheeks were rosy and he was rubbing his hands together. It must be really cold out there. I remembered that he had scheduled a walkabout to show me the property and I was glad I had donned sturdy shoes.

"It must be a cold morning. Would you like a warm-up? I can give you hot tea. And toast and jam if you'd like."

He accepted my offer and sat down at the table. "This is like old times. Mr. Willy was always ready with second breakfast on a chilly morning." I detected a tear glistening in his eye.

My breakfast conversation dwelt on my successes with Hobo. "I think he wants a full bowl of chow morning and evening, and I've learned how to interpret his in-out barks. He came upstairs to guard the bedroom while I slept. Is a rug in the bedroom door his usual bed? Do you think I'm treating him right?"

"He was probably grateful for the company and to be back in the house in the company of an occupant. I only feed him one bowl of chow once a day, Mr. Willy gave him half a bowl twice a day. I shut him in the barn at night because there are coyotes in the woods; he has a flapper door to let him in and out. I get along with him OK; he's used to me. But I'm sure he hasn't given his heart to me. Maybe he won't soon commit to anyone. Mr. Willy talked to him a lot, sort of person to person. Maybe if you did the same, it would help build a bond. I think you will have to be patient."

I was dubious. Hobo had displayed neither animosity toward nor interest in me. He just tolerated me and my clumsy attempts to attend to his needs. Andy put down his empty cup.

"How about that walk? Be sure to put on a warm jacket. If you didn't bring one, Mr. Willy kept one hanging in the powder room and I haven't had the heart to get rid of any of his things. If you stay, that will be up to you."

Mr. Willy's jacket had a sheepskin lining and smelled of Hai Karate. Despite bright sunlight, that jacket was a welcome defense against the early morning cold. I noticed a skim of ice on the puddles we skirted down by the barn. The dogwood knew it was Spring but Bald Knob as a whole was reluctant to admit it. We started our walk by touring the barn where Andy kept the machinery he used to groom areas around the buildings. A partition separated the generator and the propane tank from the storage areas. I caught a glimpse of a car behind another partition. Hobo displayed a brief proprietary interest in a cozy little stall filled with hay but he didn't linger. He stayed close to Andy and me as we followed the paths around the house and barn. When we ranged farther, Andy dismissed him with the words, "OK, have fun" and he began to frolic, running in circles around the two of us, bucking and kicking up his heels in a mockery of our sedate pace. I could have sworn I saw a broad grin spread over his face and that the deployment of his lolloping tongue was a hearty laugh.

"He loves to walk and play fetch with his toys but I haven't had much time for it since Mr. Willy passed." Andy spoke in apology.

It wasn't long before our pace over the uneven ground had me sweating. The trees were lacy with tiny buds beginning to leaf out and I could imagine that in another week or so, the paths we trod would be shaded under thick foliage. Here and there bare bones of the stony knob pushed up through patches of leaf mold. Off to the sides, tiny pale-pink flowerets lifted shy heads and an occasional purple patch of violets stood in contrast to dead leaves that had sheltered them from snow and frost. Sprigs of green dotted the ground under bushes so far leafless. Andy commented: "Another week and May apples and trilliums will be out. Wild plants in these woods run thick wherever there's a bit of soil for their roots. Mr.

Willy never had any intentions to make gardens around the house. Said no landscaping could match what God planted out here under the trees."

After slogging through a dense growth of bushes and trees, we came to a clearing that was all rock, weathered and split and treacherous underfoot. An outcrop reared high above a ledge that formed a rough bench at its foot. Bright green tufts of grass poked up from crevices. With a gesture Andy suggested we sit down. A magnificent panorama of heights and valleys, seemingly limitless, spread in front of our vantage point. Andy began to indicate points of interest: a plume of smoke that gave away the location of Ma Baker's holding at the dead end of Hudson Road; a speck of red roof that marked the roof of Corona's general store; a distant sphere on the horizon that was the water tower for Greenwood, the next town on the road through Corona. Greenwood was the place to go for groceries that Burr Worman didn't carry. Ma Baker was the curmudgeon pottery lady, the smoke meant she had her kiln going. Andy suggested I pay her a visit if I decided to stay on Bald Knob. "She comes across pretty tough but she and Mr. Willy had long friendship marked by harmless bickering. Her family was settled on Bald Knob before the Bells, growing taters and corn in a hollow, making moonshine and hunting critters in the woods. She's the only one left and she must get awfully lonely. Might be glad to see you."

We rose and went on, no paths any more, just bare rock that led down and around to a series of ledges above a narrow green meadow where red and white cows grazed contentedly. The ledges came to an end on a hogback ridge cut by a path beaten in the dirt by the wheels of Andy's ATV. I begged for a rest, I wasn't used to walking broken ground. Andy laughed and offered me a stump with a flat top. When I had caught my breath and began to look around, Andy pointed out his house, a tiny cottage located on flat ground beside the brook that ran from the heights to the meadow where the cows fed. The dirt road by the stump started at the cottage and ran across the ridge and down out of sight until it came to another little meadow next to Mr. Willy's barn.

"For a city girl you do pretty well; you've stuck it out for a five-mile walk with no complaints. It's not far to the house. I vote we get back, hunt up Mr. Willy's coffee pot and his can of coffee, dig out one of his Sweep-the-Kitchen pizzas from the freezer, and have lunch. I'll cook and you can watch."

I took his compliment at face value and reciprocated with another proposal. "It's a deal. I saw a package of Oreos in the pantry that we can crack for dessert."

We chatted companionably over lunch. I learned that Andy was born in the Netherlands but when he was six his parents divorced. His father had won custody and when he was engaged as a landscape designer for gardens at Winterthur, Biltmore, and similar grand estates, he brought his son along to the U.S. Life and schooling in the U.S. explained Andy's fluent, accent-free English. He had been studying animal husbandry at Purdue University when his father died and he was obliged to return to the Netherlands. Meeting Cousin Willy won his sponsorship for readmission to the U.S. With a small inheritance, he had then bought abandoned land next to Mr. Willy's. He applied for citizenship and sent for his Dutch fiancée. However, when she saw how remote his homestead was from bright lights and busy streets she dumped him and headed back to Amsterdam.

Too bad, I said but Andy shrugged. "It was a mistake to ask her over. The cottage was more than half a ruin and the cows were the only living things besides me that Gerda had to talk to. I've since fixed up the cottage and it now suits me quite well. My cattle business prospers. I've made friends, Mr. Willy foremost, and he taught me to look after myself. I bake a mean loaf of bread and do wonders with ground beef, thanks to a Better Homes and Gardens cookbook he gave me. If you stay, I'll invite you to dinner sometime just to prove it." As he talked, I was thinking how engaging his smile and sparkling eyes were, how pleasant his voice was, and how much I was beginning to like him. If I stayed at Bald Knob, I was sure I would enjoy knowing him.

After he left, I washed up the dishes by hand. There was a dishwasher but no point in firing it up for the few dishes I would dirty with hit-and-miss dining. I had my eye on an evening meal—roast beef pictured on a Swanson package in the freezer. My expectations of a packaged TV dinner were not high, but cooking meals from scratch for a two-day stay was not on my agenda.

I spent most of the rest of the day exploring the house. The rooms on the first floor were really elegantly appointed—not by Cousin Willy, but by an interior decorator operating with a carte blanche checkbook. Cousin Willy, in spite of his reputed intelligence, business acumen, and engineering knowhow was a typical male when he undertook to decorate his home. Stand back and pay someone to do it. When I contemplated living here, I foresaw gathering up and storing glam accessories by the boxful. In my exploration I had been to the basement and been pleased to find boo-coo storage space and laundry facilities. I imagined keeping and using everything I found in the kitchen; the appliances, pots, pans, cutlery, and dishware were ample, well-chosen, and top of the line. While I mentally redid this room or that, I was continually reminding myself I was **not** committed to sign that contract and make a home on Bald Knob. As far as Hobo was concerned, nothing seemed likely to prevent co-existence. I told myself we might learn to like one another. So far our relationship, although far from warm, was promising. I kept reminding myself that I didn't want to commit myself to living on Bald Knob with only Hobo for company. And furthermore, I didn't want or need a salary of $10,000 a month so badly that I was willing to overlook the disadvantages I saw in meeting the terms of the contract. Still, it would be nice to pay off my car and credit card balance, maybe even get a better and more reliable car, maybe invest in a smart new wardrobe. I couldn't remember a time in my life when I had disposable income of more than a couple hundred dollars. I was still wandering around the house, turning my quandary over in my mind, when I realized it was time to put the TV dinner in the oven.

Contrary to my expectations, Swanson's roast beef dinner was quite tasty. With no dishes to wash I went to Cousin Willy's office and tried the recliner/TV combination. I tuned into an episode of *Nova* featuring spectacular volcanic eruptions and watched entranced. I didn't know whether it was the technical quality of the set or the efficiency of the satellite transmission, but the picture was the best I had ever in my life seen. The pathetic little set in my apartment couldn't hold a candle (or should I say pixel) to this one. After volcanoes I switched to a rerun of *I Love Lucy* but within a few minutes I had fallen sound asleep. The comfy recliner pampered the bones and muscles wearied by the morning's five-mile walk.

I waked with a start, a cold, wet nose nudging my elbow. I glanced at my watch, 10:15, Lucy long gone. I struggled to my feet. Hobo watched me somewhat anxiously. The bones and muscles soothed by my comfortable posture had stiffened and neither he nor I seemed sure I could restore motion to my protesting body. But I did. To the tune of groans and grunts I performed my duty to Hobo and the evening ritual that addressed his needs. That accomplished, I remembered Andy's advice and locked the back door, then turned the TV off and the lights out and locked the other door. I hobbled past Hobo waiting at the foot of the stairs and limped up to the bedroom. In the bathroom I ran a warm, almost hot bath in the spa tub, dumped in some scented bubble bath that I had found in the linen closet, and turned on the agitation. While I spent 20 minutes up to my neck in aromatic aqua-massage in the tub, I observed Hobo retrieving his rug from under the bed where I had returned it that morning. By the time I was able to climb from the tub, don my pajamas, and swallow two aspirins, he was curled up and sleeping peacefully. I didn't curl up but I followed his example on the firm mattress and smooth sheets of Cousin Willy's bed.

I woke the next morning at dawn. I was still stiff but another soak in the spa loosened me up considerably. Hobo was downstairs, affable but not affectionate, ready for food and his morning outing. After I had breakfasted, I went to Cousin Willy's office to tune into a TV news program. I found one that I watched from the desk chair. It was a waste of time, the talking heads were still chewing over Congressional squabbles and massacres of civilians in war zones and Arab food markets.

A sudden and shocking insight almost took my breath away. If I signed that dratted contract, I would be obliged to spend eight months out of the year here in this house on this mountaintop with nothing to do but tend Hobo, read, watch TV, cook rinky-dink meals, do a little house work, walk a bit in the woods. I couldn't be sure that four months elsewhere— be it the French Riviera, Miami Beach, Paris, or New York City—could compensate for the boredom of a useless existence the rest of the time in the Bell house. This new notion was certainly something to think about. I wondered, how did Cousin Willy handle it? But of course, behind that locked door on the first floor, he had his work: thinking up inventions, drawing plans, building models. He probably wasn't traveling all that much around the world to trade fairs and business meetings in his later years, but he *was* working.

I was well aware that an ethical person wouldn't pry into Cousin Willy's personal spaces. But maybe his scheme to use my services to achieve his purposes had given me the right to look past his desk top into his desk drawers. My hand strayed to the pull on the top right drawer. With a mental apology I quickly opened the drawer, and just as quickly shut it when I saw the gun inside. Guns scared me. After a moment to catch my breath, I opened the next drawer. There I found a hoard of ballpoint pens and mechanical pencils bearing the names and logos of hundreds of manufacturers and suppliers—loot from all those shows and meetings Cousin Willy must have attended, thousands of items, and probably all with their ink dried up or leads crumbled. On to the next drawer, a deep one, fitted with racks to hold file folders. The folders were all neatly labeled: correspondence, Hobo, receipts, *et cetera*. Two folders contained clippings of news items that had caught Willy's eye, most of them tales of animals languishing in no-kill shelters. Often a clipping carried a Post-it note, "Sent a donation" ten, fifty, a hundred dollars. These clippings and donations had to be the reason for his scheme to ensure a normal home for Hobo after his death. Reading newspapers and sifting the news for animals in limbo was probably his pastime. I was touched but puzzled that his will had not designated animal welfare agencies as beneficiaries. Maybe he didn't believe in shotgun charity, instead thought making me personally responsible for his dog was a better solution.

I shifted my attention to the left bank of drawers. It took some muscle to pull the top one open. It proved to be packed full of identical, black-bound books, 5x 8 inches in size and a half-inch thick. I extracted what appeared to be the most recent addition. Every line of every page was filled full width with small, very precise hand-printing. Only occasionally was there a date and the book I selected was only two-thirds full. I turned to the last complete pages and began to read. Cousin Willy had composed a journal, random thoughts, not necessarily expressed grammatically or in complete sentences and rarely dated.

The entries I read rambled. Sometimes they were memories of days of his youth or achievements; Hobo's current antics were favorite grist, as were sightings of a hawk soaring, a visit with Ma Baker "the old witch." When I turned back to much earlier pages, a reference to prowlers, "I don't think my stuff is an easy target for industrial espionage. Hankins has had an eye on Bald Knob for a long time." About twenty pages further on, "I got off a shot at Hankins's goon. Think that will discourage more visits." Ten pages before the last entry, "Report on Rebecca is back from PI. She's likely to think I've lost my marbles. Doesn't matter. She's a real Bell and right for the house. Just hope she's right for Hobo." Bottom of that page, "Drove to C to wind up my arrangements with O. I think he's got it straight about the patents and licenses. As long as they keep bringing in money, it don't matter what happens with them. Don't like to admit it but the trip just about wiped me out." Next page, "Hope Rebecca likes Andy. He's been a good friend to me and could be to her. What if she don't sign the contract? O will have some work on his hands and a lot of dough in his pockets." The last page ended with "One of these nights I'm going to go to sleep and not wake up. But that's OK, 97 years is enough to burden God's earth with my carcass."

My impression of Cousin Willy as a quirky old man had grown into admiration of his acute intelligence and meticulous mind for his work.

But other than Hobo, he didn't seem to take much stock in personal relationships and obviously I was just a happenstance. If I wanted to know him better, I'd be obliged to read a lot more of his journal and go a lot further back on its timeline. Maybe I ought to sign the contract just to have the opportunity to do that.

The second and third drawers on the left held a disorganized mess of letters and snapshots dated over a span of thirty or forty years but ending twenty five years ago. The bits I read shed no light on Willy's correspondence with my mother but likely wouldn't until I had a chance to read the journal and go through this stuff carefully. Maybe Cousin Willy's writings would cast some light on my origins, an additional reason to sign that contract. Mysteries to solve—hints of industrial espionage; the history of my parentage; the life of William G. Bell—might be a powerful antidote to boring life on Bald Knob.

Hobo was stretched out in a doze. But I had a sudden yearning for fresh air. When I said, "Wanna go for a walk, Hobo?" he leaped to his feet, ears pricked and tail a-wag.

I grabbed up Willy's jacket from the powder room. Unlocking the back door, I stepped out into a nippy morning under a sunny sky decorated with shifting wisps of cloud. The crowd of cows in the lower meadow shouldered one another for access to a trough of something. Two adult deer stood tentatively waiting for a space. Andy's ATV was just starting up the road that led to his cottage. I waved but I was sure he hadn't seen me. Hobo was choosing the route for our walk. He coaxed me into a narrow passage between two dense ranks of evergreens where I would not have chosen to go if he had not been so insistent. About fifty feet down the path, the gloom suddenly opened to a wide grass-grown area, sunlit and studded with fifteen or twenty stubby limestone pillars. Graveyard immediately came to mind and when I started to inspect the pillars, by golly, they *were* gravestones. I wandered among them idly reading the names and dates carved on them: One, circled by several small slabs, bore the single word HOBO, no dates on any of them. Others identified Bells mostly, some Millmans, one or two Bakers, with dates beginning in 1820. Another standing over a small patch of earth mulched with pine needles bore the name William George Bell, and the date February 4, 2011. Cousin Willy's final resting place. I knelt for a moment to pay my respects. Hobo joined me, stretching out one paw to pat at the mulch, as if to say "Hello, old pal." I wondered what was going through his mind.

When I got to my feet, Hobo started to lead again, this time on a steeply winding downhill path into a ravine where a stream flowed into a small body of water, obviously the millpond that once had fed the grist mill lying in ruins beside it. A flock of ducks paddled busily on the pond's surface, upending to dredge green plants from under the water—a peaceful scene until Hobo dashed joyously into the water to send ducks flying in all directions. He returned to my side for a hearty shake, then looked up to my face as if to say "Great sport, and my duty's done." To which I replied, "And it's time to go back to the house." The ascent was rather demanding and I was breathless by the time we reached the top. We finished the walk with a leisurely circuit of the house and barn. Hobo enjoyed himself by darting into every patch of tall grass or shrubby growth to investigate for small prey, mice maybe. When we got into the house, we stopped in the office for a nap.

But my mind was too busy for sleep, occupied by a zillion thoughts. I tried to put them in order in preparation for my next conversation with Daniel O'Leary. Tomorrow morning I intended to tackle that treacherous hillside track down to Corona and the less strenuous trip back to Shady Grove. Once in Shady Grove, I would call the offices of Bocce, O'Leary, and Shapiro, ask for our Miss Bain, and get an appointment with the great man. I didn't yet know what I was going to tell him but I had determined I would reach a decision by the time I faced him across that shining expanse of expensive desk. It wasn't fair to him or to me to put off an answer. The Bells who had lived and died here, and Hobo for whom I was developing a sincere regard, needed to know.

That evening I punched the number one key on Cousin Willy's cell phone. Andy's answer was prompt and cordial. "Hi! What can I do for you?"

"Tomorrow morning I'm heading for Shady Grove. I intend to have an answer for O'Leary within few days of my return. I'll leave Hobo outdoors and the back door unlocked when I take off. If that's OK?"

"Sure. Don't worry about Hobo or the house. I'll be over by 8 A.M."

"I'll be gone by then. I want to get an early start. I'll take the used linens down to the laundry room and have all the dishes washed up and leftovers in the fridge. Will it be OK if I keep Cousin Willy's cell phone and charger?"

"Sure. But I hope you bring it back soon."

I thought that was as good as an invitation, whatever I decided. The next morning, I had my bags packed and the bedroom and kitchen tidied before I let Hobo out. I had finished breakfast when I let him in again. He seemed to sense that today was different. He stood motionless in perfect show style in the middle of the kitchen, his gaze trained on me as I drank the last of my tea. I had to admire his appearance: the calmly intelligent face, pricked ears, straight strong back and heavily muscled haunches. His coloring was an exact match to the example of his breed pictured in Cousin Willy's *Book of Dogs*: fawn throat, chest, and belly; black back and curving tail. I confided my admiration out loud. Since yesterday, he seemed to invite me to talk to him.

"You're a handsome fellow and I'm sure you could be my really good friend. I'm going to miss you."

He responded by coming over to me and laying his muzzle on my thigh—our first physical contact and just as I was going away. The lump in my throat didn't go away until I was in the car and driving down the lane.

Fast forward to noon, April 26, and I was turning off Hudson Road at the red Bell mailbox. My flashy new red Jeep Cherokee, detailed in gold, had taken the twists and turns that brought me here like a trooper. The car was loaded to the roof with my worldly goods and huge bags of groceries that I had purchased in Greenwood. That I was here was not a necessarily a dream come true but it was truly a dilemma put to rest.

On April 6 I had walked into O'Leary's office and blurted out, "I'm signing that contract. But I've got to have a more reliable car if I'm to live on Bald Knob."

O'Leary grinned and waved me over to his desk. "Do you understand the terms?"

"Yes," I said. "Where's the pen?"

"Within 10 minutes I had committed myself to Bald Knob for Hobo's lifetime. O'Leary, however, still had some details to address.

"Is there a landline up there?"

"I have Mr. Willy's cell...."

"If there's not a landline already, I'll get one for you. You remember that all of the Bell homestead expenses will be met by the trust working out of this office. We need to have reliable communications for the instructions we will have for you and the questions you will have for us. Our Mr. Bender will be your usual contact." He shuffled some papers and went on. "This afternoon your first month's salary, $10,000, will be in the First National Bank of Columbia. Stop by the Shady Grove branch tomorrow to pick up your checkbook." He raised his voice to a genteel shout. "Mrs. Devlin, ask Mr. Bender in."

I nodded, speechless and overwhelmed by O'Leary's rush of words. When Mr. Bender arrived, he proved to be middle-aged, short, a bit pudgy, and furnished with an engaging smile. O'Leary introduced him. "Ben, get a voucher ready for Miss Bell to take with her. Make it good for any car dealership in Columbia so she'll be able to negotiate a trade-in of her old car against the paid-up purchase of a new one, yet today if she would like...."

I timidly ventured, "A four-wheel drive? Something like a Jeep?"

"Whatever you want. I've only made one trip up that road to the Bell homestead and it definitely calls for four-wheel drive. Oh, and if you want household help, Ben here can arrange that for you. Mr. Bell had a standing order for cleaners every four weeks."

I walked out of the offices of Bocce, O'Leary, and Shapiro with my head in a whirl. When I could think straight again, I drove down the street to the dealer with the most Jeeps in his front lot. I could hardly believe that I didn't have to kick tires or haggle to get a brand-new vehicle with options like a CD player, GPS, and leather seats. On top of that, the dealer could arrange the insurance and license application before I drove away. I arrived at the Bell mailbox with my new car crammed to the roof with my new wardrobe I had purchased after paying off all my outstanding bills. I was determined to make a clean start on Bald Knob. Clothes I had for teaching school were not at all suitable to country living, so extra jeans, shirts, shorts, and additional pairs of stout shoes accounted for most of the new outfits.

When I drove into the parking area, Andy and Hobo were waiting. Andy came toward me with a handshake, Hobo went into an undignified display—galloping in circles, kicking up his heels, throwing himself down on his back inviting a belly rub.

"What's wrong with him?"

Andy was laughing. "He's glad to see you back. So am I but I'm behaving better. Hobo, sit!"

The dog calmed down and sat panting, his emotions controlled but not eliminated. I was gratified and a bit embarrassed by his welcome. I wasn't sure I deserved it.

"Let's get your stuff into the house. I see you stopped at the A&P in Greenwood. Don't trust Worman's fare?"

I explained that I needed to stock up on fruit and vegetables and considering what I had seen of Worman's store, I thought it best to buy elsewhere. When Andy asked how I intended to dispose of the contents of the car, I told him the brown bags go to the kitchen, the foot locker and suitcases go to Cousin Willy's bedroom, and the boxes of books stay just inside the door in the big room. "I'll get to them as I settle in."

Andy had to inspect the Jeep Cherokee before he started helping with its load. He approved. "Let me tell you, lady. This is some spiffy buggy. I would never have pegged you for such flashy ride or such neat options. The four-wheel drive is an excellent choice, especially for winter weather."

We trailed into the house, Hobo at our heels. While Andy got the foot locker and suitcases upstairs, I unloaded the brown bags and stowed items in the refrigerator and freezer. I was hungry after my early start from Shady Grove. I asked Andy if he would like a late lunch, by now it was 2:30. Sure, he said, and I made a salad and broke out one of the superduper frozen pizzas. Andy disappeared into the basement and returned with a bottle of Chardonnay.

"I'll bet you hadn't found the wine cellar yet. It's a real cave and there's beer down there too. Mr. Willy liked a glass of beer or wine with his dinner most days."

I was pleased that Hobo, although he had lost his ebullience, still stayed close to me. He was at my knee as I sat down to the table; he didn't beg, he simply acted like he wanted to be where I was. I was flattered no end, but surprised. I didn't think that our previous two-and-a-half days of companionship had been long enough to bond and I didn't know how he knew I was here to stay. When I said so, Andy had an explanation. "You fed and watered him and you slept in Mr. Willy's bed. Those were maybe major factors, but I suspect that not pushing him into a relationship helped. He wanted, I think, to make the first moves and I'm sure he appreciated your low-key ways. It took him a whole lot longer to accept me after Mr. Willy was gone and I had known him since he was a pup."

As we ate and chatted, Andy told me he had cleared space in the barn so I could put up my car out of the weather. He had got a complete set of the keys on Mr. Willy's ring made for me. But he warned me. "There were keys on Mr. Willy's ring that I couldn't match to locks. I tagged likely ones on your ring but you'll have the fun of figuring out the rest. I hope you don't mind but I'd like to keep the set I've been using. O'Leary called me and engaged me to continue my services to the estate as before.

I need many of the keys for the outbuildings and equipment. If I were you, I'd leave Mr. Willy's workrooms locked and undisturbed. Mr. Willy's car is in the barn and its keys are still on the ring. But I can't recommend driving it. He let the tires go bald and didn't keep the oil changed—said he wasn't going to waste money on it since he likely wouldn't outlast it. It's a 1950 Buick sedan with 250,000 miles on the odometer. You might get something for it at an antique car auction."

I told Andy I'd be quite comfortable with him having keys to everything on the Bell homestead. I also asked him if he knew anything about Mr. Willy's computer. I would like to use it but I was nervous in the first place about invading Cousin Willy's privacy and secondly I was such a computer klutz that I feared I might inadvertently damage its programs and files. Andy gave me the phone number for the GEEK he used for his computer problems. He said the guy was bonded to be confidential and was also a very competent instructor for an amateur user.

It was getting on for twilight before Andy went home, and there was nothing left of the salad, the pizza, or the wine in the bottle. We had had a very pleasant afternoon. Hobo didn't even see Andy to the door; he was still sticking close to me. I found his devotion heartwarming. In my whole life, I had never had a pet or an animal friend.

The days on Bald Knob rolled by pleasantly. I had never realized nor valued lessons I learned teaching at Shady Grove High School. I had hated the monthly sessions we teachers were obliged to attend to work on teaching skills. But by golly, I had learned from them: to get a good sleep every night; to rise at the same time every morning; to get to work at the same time every day; to have a plan for the activity of the day and a goal to achieve by the end of it; and to organize my free time to accomplish all the chores that needed to be done in a timely fashion. Now I applied what I had learned about time and materials management to life on Bald Knob. I got up at six, breakfasted while Hobo made his morning round, put the kitchen in order, listened to 30 minutes of TV news (I had purchased a small TV for the kitchen) and then tackled the morning's scheduled job: laundry, dusting and vacuuming, a trip down the mountain for groceries or shopping, and preparations for the meal that would generate leftovers for the next several days. After lunch, a walk with Hobo on the trails he chose (often a demanding but always diverse exercise) was followed by the job scheduled for the afternoon: moving furniture, sorting through desk drawers and assessing contents; two hours weekly with the GEEK and practicing daily assigned computer tutorials; and exploration of odd corners of the house. Reading and TV viewing were reserved for evenings although I often fell asleep early after a particularly busy day.

Moving furniture was key to my giving that big empty front room a purpose. I left the cluster of leather seating around the fireplace but I dragged an area rug from one of the sitting rooms to the remaining space and lugged occasional chairs, tables, and lamps from other rooms into attractive positions. On one of Andy's unlucky days, I caught him at the barn and enlisted his help to move in two large divans. He taught me a trick (I presume to save him from similar future tasks) for moving heavy pieces. I found I could lift a corner or two of a big piece onto a rug and then tow the rug and its load over the smooth wood floors to a new location. That worked as long as the piece was small enough to go through the doors on the way. I brought home empty boxes from the A&P and Sunday newspapers from Monday shopping trips for wrapping up excessive decorator's furbelows and stowing them away. After a month of such endeavors, the front room and the downstairs casual rooms looked like places to live in instead of showrooms. Andy approved of my rearrangements until I asked him to help me carry boxes down to storage in the basement. Some of my choices of box size had been unwise, proof of the old saw about eyes being bigger than capacity, in this instance weight limit.

I found time to have Andy to a home-cooked meal at least once a week. If I do say so, I'm a pretty fair cook, thanks to Mary Conrad's patient coaching. Andy would arrive in chinos and an Oxford cloth shirt, with his blond hair slicked down, and smelling of Old Spice. We always had plenty to talk about; aside from reminiscences of our past lives, there were the daily events on Bald Knob and around the world. He would leave for his cottage about 8 after complimenting and thanking me at length for a great meal. For a goodnight, he had at last stopped calling me Miss Bell, but hadn't settled on Becca, Becky, Rebecca, or RJ as the favored alternative. Hobo would accompany him to the door for a final caress and then follow me back to the kitchen for a treat and a post mortem on the evening. Andy was a good listener but Hobo as a good listener had limited staying power. A huge yawn signaled maximum disinterest.

I had had many phone conversations with Mr. Bender and had made two trips in to the offices of B.O.&S. to sign papers. Although I had added a scanner/copier to Cousin Willy's office equipment, I thought a FAX machine would be overkill. So far matters had gone smoothly. The landline phone was in, the process watched intently by Hobo. The tech was nervous, fearful that Hobo's attitude boded attack. But after I reassured him and commanded Hobo to sit and stay on the veranda, he relaxed. The cleaners retained by Cousin Willy, and continued by Mr. Bender had come once and massaged my ego by praising the changes I had made. Hobo accepted their presence as a matter of course. I made a note to remember that Hobo's attitudes toward strangers on the place were mixed blessings. The kind he tolerated were those he had known of old.

41

The occupations of those early days of life on the Bell homestead taught me my way around the house and the land. My sense of belonging grew stronger with each passing day. Since Hobo was my constant companion, I bonded to him more closely than I ever had to any human. Indoors or out, he was with me, supremely companionable, but never a nuisance. In mid-June I had evidence of his protective abilities. On one of our favorite walks we rounded a blind curve and surprised a man wearing camouflage clothing and toting a rifle. He was heavily bearded and none too clean. A vagrant gust of wind carried the smell of stale beer and overtired underwear in my direction. Hobo planted himself stiff-legged in front of me, hackles raised, and voiced a growl like rolling thunder. The man swung his rifle around, not quite pointing it but certainly making a threatening gesture.

"Watch your dog, lady. He ain't actin' friendly," he yelled.

I yelled back. "That's because you are on my land without permission. Trespass and hunting are not allowed, signs are posted all around. You have ignored them. Now I suggest you get back to the road and leave the area!"

Instead of retreating, the man took a step toward us. Hobo's growl turned into a single warning bark before he bared his teeth and began to move slowly toward the intruder.

"Call off your dog, I'm telling you." His bluster had no effect on Hobo's slow approach. The man was finally convinced of his risk and turned to go away. A few yards down the path, he stopped briefly and waved his gun a couple of times, then picked up his pace and was soon out of sight.

"Do you think we should follow this guy? Or is discretion the better part of valor?" I asked Hobo. He continued to growl but stood still and turned his head toward me as if waiting for instructions. I gave them but they specified going back the way we had come. When we reached a rocky outcrop that overlooked the lower part of the path, I climbed up for a view. The man was just pushing his way through the brush toward a battered pickup parked on Hudson Road. I tried to memorize the appearance of man and vehicle in case I decided to report his encroachment to the sheriff. When I told Andy of the incident, he said reporting would probably be a waste of breath but do it, if it would make me feel better. I let it go and rewarded Hobo with extra treats for his vigilance.

A season of thunderstorms began. Spectacular lightning strikes hit Bald Knob with every storm but strategically placed lightning rods prevented damage to the buildings. One strike took down a big old poplar across the lane and I had to call Andy to bring his chain saw to reopen the way. I thought maybe I would have a batch of firewood as a result but Andy said the wood was too green. He cut up the trunk and stacked the chunks in a pile next to the drive.

"If you want to use the fireplace in the living room, there's a bunch of dry wood Mr. Willy had split and stowed under the veranda. Just have to carry it in. My advice is to not carry in more than you plan to burn at a time. Otherwise you might have some unwelcome insect life to deal with."

I took his advice. Once I had discovered how to work the dampers, I found chilly post-thunderstorm evenings in front of a glowing hearth were well worth the work of lugging in the fuel. Andy came over once in a while to join me and Hobo for popcorn and talk. Sometimes he brought his DVD player and hooked it up to the 45 inch flat-screen TV I had bought for the living room where there was already an outlet. I was enjoying the self-indulgence I could buy with my humongous salary. Other than the few appliance purchases and the GEEK's fee, my purchases for groceries, gas, and an occasional piece of replacement underwear seldom made a perceptible dent in my bank account.

One fine afternoon in July when I said to Hobo "We ought to visit our neighbor," he responded enthusiastically. I didn't know much about her, only that she was called Ma Baker and said to be crazy. Andy told me she lived at the dead end of Hudson Road, about three quarters of a mile beyond the Bell mailbox. "Don't try your pretty red Jeep past your mailbox or you'll end up with a broken axle. The road deteriorates into bottomless potholes, crevices, and chasms. The post office refuses to deliver mail up there so she uses Burr Worman's store for an address."

"How does she get her groceries?"

"She walks down a secret trail. The slope is not as steep as Hudson Road but I suspect it's just as challenging. Mr. Willy is probably the only one who knew it. He used to go over to check on her after a big snow."

"Age 97?" My amazement was boundless.

Andy shrugged. "He was a tough old bird and physically able until the last couple months of his life. She's another tough old bird although she's at least 15 years younger than he was."

My curiosity was at a high pitch as I started out in the car, Hobo riding shotgun. I parked and locked the car at the mailbox and we tackled the gullies and tumbled slabs of rock that passed for a road. It took almost an hour and about all my stamina to reach a clearing at the end. Even Hobo seemed winded.

A ramshackle house and a barn in fairly good repair stood in the clearing. A huge stack of firewood leaned on one wall of the barn. Ma Baker's kiln was a beehive-shaped pile of logs cunningly interwoven to let air through while keeping fierce heat in. A woman I presumed was Mrs. Baker was standing in front of the kiln, hands on hips, gazing intently at its interior glow.

"Hello," I called.

She whirled and the skirts of her full length dress fanned out to show the heavy farm boots on her feet. She was a woman of middle size, brown and wizened as one of last year's apples forgotten and left to dry on the tree. She wore her white hair skinned back into a skimpy knot on the top of her head. She fastened a grey-eyed gaze as piercing as paired stilettos on me.

"You got to be Rebecca Bell. Willy said I'd see you one day when curiosity got the better of you."

"How did he know I'd come to Bald Knob to live?"

"He knew. He fixed it so you couldn't not come. Come here, Hobo. Don't hang back. Cassandra is in the house."

"Who's Cassandra?" I asked.

"Twenty pounds of meanness. My cat and sworn enemy of Hobo. Come over here and have a seat on this bench. I got to stay and watch the fire, got to keep it just right for this batch of pots."

Hobo stayed by my side as I approached the bench, but kept a wary eye on the house. Ma Baker picked up a jug, filled a shallow bowl with water, and set it down for Hobo. She settled on the bench and patted a spot where I was to sit. Hobo snuggled up to my feet. He was scared! That cat must be a hellion.

"How's it goin'? You been lonesome or is Andy's company keeping you entertained?"

"Hobo is good company. I only see Andy a couple times a week. He's busy with his cows."

"Uh huh. Well, you be nice to him. He was Willy's good friend and he can be yours. You been seein' any strangers in the woods lately?"

"A guy that might have been a stray hunter. I had to order him off the property."

"He wasn't no hunter. He's a scout lookin' for a place in these woods to set up one of them militia camps. You see him again, get the sheriff after him. Him and his friends are bad news." She broke off suddenly and dashed over to the kiln to rearrange some fiery embers with a long steel rod.

When she took her seat again, she said "Name's Eugenia, my mother called me Genie, and everyone else around here calls me Ma. You can call me whatever you want. I hear tell Willy's lawyers call you the 'tenant and caretaker' of the Bell estate. But Willy told me how he was gonna rope you in. I told him it was a sneaky deal, getting a young woman to waste her youth up here on the top of nowhere. But he just laughed and said the girl is a real Bell, she'll make out OK. Are you makin' out OK?"

"Yes, so far. But what made him think I was a real Bell and could handle the job he had cut out for me?"

"I don't know, maybe because he knew your mother and how she toughed out the scandal."

"What scandal? I've been looking through Cousin Willy's papers and haven't found any evidence of a scandal, unless it was my illegitimacy."

"Keep looking, you'll find it. Willy never told me the whole of it but he said he had it all written down. You'll find it. Hey, my pots are about to need all my attention, can't spare time to talk any more. Come back some other time. You'll always be welcome."

She jumped up and grabbed her steel rod and began to stir around in the embers. I took my dismissal in good part, there would be another time to visit.

"'Bye, Mrs. Eugenia," I called as I started to leave the clearing. Hobo was still sticking close. Cassandra the cat must be a real bugaboo if she worried my fearless companion so much. It took less than an hour to get back to my car since I already knew the worst of the pitfalls on that horrible thoroughfare. Mrs. Baker's reference to a scandal had made me eager to continue searching Cousin Willy's papers.

For the next few days I concentrated on sifting through the photos and letters in the bottom desk drawer. I finally found four undated letters from my mother and a black and white photograph of a little girl in a frilly dress carrying an Easter basket. The letters dealt with commonplaces like going to church and the weather. "Becca, 4" was written on the back of the photo. I was already tall and skinny at age 4 but my hair was long and wavy, lying on my shoulders. My face was all eyes and prim, partially toothless smile. I knew the next step in my hunt for family history was in Cousin Willy's journals. But it wouldn't be easy since he didn't date his entries and when he did, the date rarely included the year.

I gave up after another session of unsuccessful rummage and invited Hobo to go for a walk. He led me enthusiastically down a trail that was new to me. Almost obliterated by dense undergrowth on either side, it dipped precipitously into a ravine and then rose by way of switchbacks on rocky ledges to an elevation that seemed to exceed that of Bald Knob. I scrambled along after Hobo hoping he would run out of steam before I did. The trail ended on the highest level in a stone-studded clearing from which woods and sky opened in a wide panorama. It took me a moment to realize that the distance we had traveled was almost entirely vertical and that the apex of the trail was less than a mile from Corona by crow flight. Looking down, I could see almost every building in the town.

A growing interest in the wildlife of the Bell property had accustomed me to hang Cousin Willy's excellent binoculars around my neck when Hobo and I walked the trails. Now I lifted them to my eyes and focused casually on Burr Worman's general store and a battered pickup parked in front. As I watched, Burr and two men emerged from the store and went to stand by the vehicle which I now recognized from my earlier encounter with the trespasser. In the heat of the day the two men with Burr had shed their shirts, but their khaki undershirts and camouflage pattern pants caught my eye especially. Broad visors on their caps more or less concealed their faces but a bush of hair escaped the cap of the man whose build and height most resembled those of my trespasser. The arms and shoulders of the other man were covered with tattoos. Except for a large red swastika on the biceps of the man's right arm, the figures were rather indistinct. The men were engaged in lively conversation accompanied by vigorous arm waving. Burr was more composed and seemed to listen more often than talk. Remembering Ma Baker's caution about such strangers, I set myself to memorize the few distinguishing characteristics I could make out. Suddenly the two men abruptly terminated their tirades, flung themselves into the pickup, and left the lot in a cloud of dust. Burr stood for a minute or two shaking his head, and then went back into the store.

I called to Hobo who sat patiently waiting for me in the only shade available on the peak and together we started down. I hadn't been afraid on the steep approach but going down brought my heart into my mouth. The ascent on far side of the ravine was a cakewalk compared to that fearful descent but all the same I was breathing hard when we reached a familiar cross trail that brought us home. Andy was putting up the mower when I hailed him from the parking lot. I was bursting with my news. I told him of my visit to Ma Baker and her warning and of the event I had just witnessed. "I'd say the man with the tattoos was about five-six and other one six even. Both of them were white, but tanned, and had dark hair but there was gray in what I could see of the tall one's hair and beard. The tall one had a wide leather belt with a bright metal buckle but the other one wore a plain belt and buckle. Their footgear was heavy boots, high-laced; they looked very military.

Andy listened impassively as I told my tale but when I finished, he asked me if I had my cell phone along. No, I said, I don't carry it on walks. Whereupon he whipped out his phone, punched in some numbers, and said "Tell the girl who answers your full name, Bald Knob, and what you just told me."

I obeyed. The female who answered didn't waste words. "I've recorded everything. Expect a call or visit from the Special Deputy within the next four hours. Thank you for calling." CLICK. As I handed Andy his phone back, I asked, "What's this all about?"

"The sheriff has set up a special division to work all sightings of the kind of guys you've described. The word has it that they are part of a citizen's militia group looking for a campsite. The Special Deputy will want to question you, Ma Baker, and Burr. So don't be surprised or worried when you hear from him or her."

"Whew! Should I be taking special precautions when Hobo and I walk? Cousin Willy had a handgun in his desk drawer but I wouldn't know the first thing about defending myself with it." My knees were shaking but I managed to sound calm.

"Tomorrow I'll come over and give you some lessons. HOWEVER, and let me emphasize it, DON'T CARRY THE GUN WITH YOU. You're more likely to hurt yourself or Hobo than you are to drive off an intruder. For now, just make sure the doors are locked when you are inside the house and that you don't answer the door for anyone but me or somebody with a badge. OK?"

"OK, but you've got me worried. I've never been afraid up here and I don't want to be from now on."

"Wait until you've talked with the Special Deputy and know more about what's going on. I'll try some of my contacts, maybe get a handle on how serious these sightings might be."

The next morning Andy came over and took me through a rigorous program to learn how a Glock 9 mm works and how it's taken apart, cleaned, and reassembled. He took me out and allowed me to load and fire it at a big old oak tree. After much coaching, I killed the tree once, wounded it twice, and missed it entirely three times. I winced with every shot but was surprised they were not much louder than car backfires. Hobo sat and watched from about thirty yards behind me. I came away from the lessons a little less fearful than before but still far from comfortable with the gun. Andy promised to supervise practice sessions until the ammunition ran out. Considering the two boxes we had found with it in the desk drawer, that would not happen for a month of Sundays.

I was clearing away the breakfast dishes when Special Deputy Roth called and told me to expect a visit around 1:30 if that was OK. Sure, I said.

The deputy's cruiser nosed into the parking area right on time. The female who stepped out was svelte in a trim gray uniform, with a thick braid of blonde hair hanging halfway down her back. She probably weighed about 130 pounds prior to putting on 50 pounds of equipment: gold insignia including her official badge; shoulder radio; wide belt with holstered gun; handcuffs; and a bulky Kevlar vest. A laminated badge dangling from a shirt button displayed rank (Deputy Sergeant), name (Lillian Roth) and an unsmiling photograph of her attractive face: blue eyes, rosy cheeks, perfect teeth, and firm chin. Hobo took her arrival in stride, although he stuck close to my side throughout her visit.

Introductions and handshakes over, we took up chairs on the veranda and Deputy Roth took out pen and notepad. I told her my story and answered a few questions, such as times of day when I encountered the intruder on the path and saw the men talking to Burr Worman. After she had wrung everything out of my memory that she could, she told me why she was a Special Deputy. She was on a task force set up to keep track of members of The Patriot Guard, a group with paramilitary pretensions, that had been run out of a neighboring county. The motto of the Patriot Guard was "Defense of Liberty;" the design on their flag superimposed a coiled rattlesnake on red-white-and-blue stripes. The task force had information that members spotted in the vicinity so far were scouting for a secluded spot to set up a clandestine camp and training ground where a local "regiment" of about 25 men would gather on weekends. There had not yet been any explicit threats to property owners in the county, but sightings around and in heavily wooded areas had become frequent and worrisome. Deputy Roth advised me to stay alert, keep my doors locked, and to call her at any time at the number on her card.

As I saw the deputy off, I was mulling a mixture of relief and trepidation: relief that law enforcement was paying attention to this bunch of radicals, trepidation lest the group cranked up their explorations. Bell land was obviously a tempting target for their purposes. It encompassed some 1600 acres of irregular topography: thick forest and mini-alps surrounding pockets of almost level land situated along small watercourses. Andy's cattle operations used only a few of the level spaces. I pulled out the cell phone and called him with my news but discovered he had already been contacted by Deputy Roth because his land (which he called a *spread*) abutted on mine and his business used parts of it. He just repeated her recommendations and suggested Hobo and I walk trails that were more distant from Hudson Road. I made up my mind to work hard on shooting skills. I didn't want to shoot anyone but if push came to shove....

On Monday, as I practiced Internet searches, Hobo rose and took a vigilant stance at the back door. I heard a knock and looked out the window to see Ma Baker carrying something bulky in a burlap sack. Hobo relaxed the moment he saw her.

"Come in, Mrs. Eugenia. You must have had a rough trip over that broken road."

"Didn't come on the road. Came by the secret way Willy and me always used. Let's open this bundle on the veranda. I felt bad about sending you away so fast the other day so I brought you a pot for a present."

When the burlap fell away from her burden, a wide-mouthed, wasp-wasted pot appeared. Glazed in black and speckled with crumbs of white limestone, it was not a simple pot, it was a work of art. I gasped in admiration and delight.

"So beautiful! I love it and I love you for the gift. Come into the living room and show me where it will look best."

"Living room, huh. I thought you'd prob'ly leave it out here on the porch. Willy would have. He'd say his decorator would think it was too hillbilly for indoors."

"Well, I'm not Willy, I appreciate art. You know, I never saw Cousin Willy and I've plowed through piles of family stuff and there's not one picture of him. What did he look like?

"Ha! Like a Bell! Like you! Like all the Bells. Very tall, lean as a greyhound, brown eyes, bony face, good teeth. Had a big thick mop of white hair. He didn't hold with pictures of himself, although some might have shown up in old trade magazines. This pot might look good on one corner of the hearth. What do you think?"

"I'll try it there but for now let's sit on this comfortable divan and talk. Do you mind me calling you Eugenia? Such a lovely name. Here's a cushion for your back. I have a lot of questions to ask you. I never met Cousin Willy so I have to ask you and Andy van Houten what he was like and why he did some of the things I find odd. Andy only knew him in the last ten, twelve years but you must have known him a lot longer."

"Sure did, grew up knowing him, but I was 15 years younger. Me and the Bell kids ran back and forth every day. I kind of like you calling me by my born name, there's no one alive any more that does. Willy called me Genie. Ask your questions and I'll answer what I can."

"Can you tell me why the log part of the house, built 100 or more years ago, has no features typical of its age? Except of course, the exterior."

"The house got changed when Willy got rich and wanted modern. His folks died or moved away during the war—that was WW II—and he wanted to make big changes. Built on that clapboard addition to hold his inventing work, and while he had contractors up here, he put them at makin' the rest of the place like places he'd seen in his travels. There was times when I'd come over and the house was just a shell, with big steel beams runnin' alongside the old hand-cut beams his granddaddy used to hold up the roof. In the 80s he started doin' things like he saw on TV. I used to tell him it was a mistake to make a silk purse out of a sow's ear. The old house wasn't no sow's ear, it had charm. Now it's probably comfortable living but it sure doesn't have charm."

I was too loyal to Cousin Willy's memory to agree with her, although I was tempted. Every day I found the hodge-podge of discordant styles less and less charming. All my efforts to move furniture around were dedicated to keeping comfort and creating a more natural style. I had made some progress but I still had a long way to go.

We chatted along until I asked her to the kitchen for tea and cookies (I had baked peanut butter nuggets the day before) and we chatted some more until she jumped to her feet and said, "Gotta go. Cat gets lonesome and she's destructive when she's lonesome."

"A couple more questions. Why is Hobo terrified of your cat? He was as brave as a lion when we were facing that intruder."

"He once walked up to Cassie to touch noses and she took it amiss. She flew into him and beat him up right and proper. He was too nice to defend himself."

I had one more question, where did she get the materials to make her pots. Her answer was quick and complete.

"Patch of clay down by the brook and fifty pounds of black slip mix I bought by mistake from a catalog years ago. Haven't used it up yet. In the meantime every piece I make gets glazed black!"

We were still chuckling when I bade her goodbye at the back door. I really liked the peppery old lady. Once I learned her special path, I'd drop in on her often.

By the middle of September I was beginning to think excitement on Bald Knob had faded. I had started to call it home. Major efforts on my part had the rooms on the first floor of the house looking like I lived in them. Computer lessons had paid off with significant success, especially in word processing. The Patriot Guard, apparently aware of the surveillance by the sheriff's task force, seemed be playing possum. Hobo and I had bonded to the point that he often read my mind. Together we often used Eugenia's special path. Although it was not a promenade, it beat the upper reach of Hudson Road by a country mile. We walked up a steep slope through dense forest to a rocky spur that dipped down within sight of Eugenia's cabin with another half mile of hard going before reaching it. The last quarter mile was difficult for Hobo. It lay inside Cassandra's prowling range and we sometimes encountered her lurking in the bushes. The cat was the size of a small dog, black as sin with four white paws and a white-tipped tail. Whenever she saw Hobo, she swelled up into a spiky ball, every hair on end, and hissed venomously. If we ignored her, and we always did, she backed off and scuttled through the brush to reach the cabin ahead of us. She provided the only threat aside from an occasional rattler that we sometimes met on our trip.

Then one morning, a sleek black limousine pulled into the parking area closest to our back veranda. Hobo bristled and barked his warning signal. I looked out the front window to see a dapper young man in an Armani suit smoothing his hair and debarking from the rear seat. My reaction was amazement that the driver of the vehicle could have navigated the twists and turns and crumbling berms of Hudson Road without incident. The young man didn't seem to have been fazed by his perilous ride. He shot the cuffs of his fine linen shirt and shrugged his jacket into shape on his shoulders before he started toward the veranda. I opened the door and stepped outside with Hobo on alert by my side.

"Miss Bell," the fellow called. "I'm glad to find you home. I would have called ahead but I had no number for you and your lawyer's office refused to furnish one. May I come in?"

"Perhaps you had better state your business." I was sure he wasn't a Patriot Guardsman, but I was cautious all the same. He looked respectable and probably was but I wasn't about to trust someone who had been turned away from the offices of B.O.&S.

"May I come up on your porch? I don't want to shout for all your neighbors to hear."

"Don't worry. Just stay where you are. I can hear you just fine."

The ingratiating smile on the guy's face faded as he began to fish in his vest pocket for a business card. When he held it out, I motioned for him to lay it on the bottom step. That forced him to tell me what the card said.

"My name is Howard Spears. I represent the Hankins Group of custom-engineered machinery. My superior, Mr. Clyde Hankins himself, sent me with a proposal. We recently learned that Mr. William Bell has died and that you, Miss Rebecca Bell, are his heir." He paused and looked expectantly at me.

"You heard wrong. I am tenant and caretaker of the Bell homestead, *not* William Bell's heir. If you or your principal wish to talk business with the Bell estate, contact the offices of Bocce, O'Leary, and Shapiro in Columbia, Indiana."

"Well, may I just come in the house and tour Mr. Bell's workrooms?"

"No, you may not. Mr. Bell's workrooms are not open for touring or any other form of entry. Now, if you will instruct your driver to return the way you came, I will bid you goodbye."

I turned and reached for the doorknob. Howard Spear's face got as red as the stripes on his silk power tie. "Wait, wait…" he babbled.

"I *could* set the dog on you." I let him consider the possibility as I turned the knob.

He considered it very quickly and scrambled through the car door. The driver started up and took the car in a long sweep around the lot and out the drive. I listened until I could no longer hear the sound of tires on gravel and then picked up Spears's card and went in to call O'Leary on the landline. He was out so I talked to Bender; I was sure he would relay the news of my visitor to O'Leary. It was not until the next day that O'Leary called back.

"Sorry for the delay in returning your call. I wanted to do some research before I filled you in. Clyde Hankins has been circling like a starved vulture waiting for your Cousin Willy to die. I'm surprised it took him so long to learn of his death. I must compliment you on your handling of Spears; it was exactly right."

"Thank you, but what's it all about? What if Spears comes back?"

"He won't. I had a talk with Clyde Hankins and he saw the light when I mentioned harassment of the Bell 'tenant and caretaker.' The reason Hankin wants a minion to get into Mr. Bell's workroom can be summed up in two words, *industrial espionage*. A procurement officer at the Pentagon let slip to someone who passed it on to Hankins that William Bell had worked out a new gadget. Mr. Bell does have a new invention going through the patent process. It's all very hush-hush but it will be worth millions to the trust in licensing fees. Hankins wants to get the scoop on it and set his engineers at pirating it before it hits the market. Hankins sells secret developments to China."

"I've seen Cousin Willy's precautions. To me they seem foolproof. The safe is massive, no one knows the combination. I can't imagine a safecracker getting through its steel and concrete shell. Cousin Willy made a joke that only Hobo knew the combination, but Hobo's not talking. So Ha! Ha! Mr. Hankins! Are you sure he'll leave me alone?"

"Not positive but almost sure. I think you still have to watch for subterfuges. For instance, bogus technical people arriving to install electronic equipment or to repair or update mechanical equipment might leave bugs behind to pick up casual conversations between you and legitimate visitors. Keep your doors locked both when you are in and when you are out of the house. Stay on the alert if you let strangers in. I *could* arrange for an alarm system but the problem with an ordinary alarm system is that a security agency couldn't respond in a timely fashion. If you decide to take time away during the winter, I can arrange for armed guards but that would probably be overkill. For the moment, I'd say the best thing to do is stay on your toes and wait to see what happens."

"I'll be frank with you. I don't like even one little bit to feel like I'm sitting on a powder keg up here, just because some pipsqueak competitor of my dead relative is trying to plunder his inventions. Do you think Hankins might try violent means to get want he wants?"

"He doesn't have a record of that, which is why I'm counseling watchful waiting. By the way, what's been happening with The Patriot Guard?"

"Deputy Roth called last week to tell me they've been lying low. I'm thankful for that."

O'Leary agreed and after a bit more chat we disconnected. I forced myself not to worry but in the deeps of the night, one minute of sleeplessness always turned into an hour of listening for unusual sounds around the house. I tried to train myself to rely on Hobo's ability to sense and warn of trouble.

I was setting aside two hours a day for time with the computer. Mike the GEEK's first visit months earlier had resolved my qualms about invading Cousin Willy's privacy. Mike had only to pop in a diagnostic floppy to determine that the hard disk had crashed several months before Willy's death and that his files couldn't be recovered. When Mike suggested replacing the hard disk (he had one in his truck) and loading current versions of programs I would probably want to use, I told him to go to it. I shed no tears over the loss of Willy's files. I was sure that he had confided more to his journal than he ever had entrusted to computer memory. Working my way gradually through the contents of those little black books had been so far interesting in general but not informative on specifics.

After Mike set me up in business with connections to the Internet and e-mail, e-mail was an unexpected boon. Burr Worman's granddaughter lived in Corona and cut men's, women's, and children's hair in her living room. She took appointments by e-mail and I had been able to avoid shagginess with only one hair-raising trip monthly down Hudson Road. I lost those golden highlights my Shady Grove salon had provided—Nell was adamant, she didn't do color!—but I looked just as good without them. She, Andy, Ben Bender, and spammers were the only e-mail correspondents I had. Spammers gave me regular opportunity to blow off steam in private profanity.

I had made considerable progress on my translation of *Les Miserables;* Jean Valjean's redemption of his sins by rescuing Fantine and Cosette had just been recorded. Although I was well-grounded in French history and geography, the Internet had proved a valuable resource for refreshing my memory on a number of points. I was about to sound out a publisher friend to gauge his interest in my efforts. Winter was coming on and if I stayed on Bald Knob I would have a lot of time for my texts.

A decision to stay on Bald Knob in winter was taking some thought. Andy thought I should exercise the time-off option in my contract to spend December to March somewhere sunny. He said snow on Hudson Road in those months was less of a danger than bitter winds, sleet, and ice. Eugenia pooh-poohed running away from weather that she had survived for 80 plus years. Her way was to put on galoshes and walk the trail to Corona for necessities. When Hobo and Ben Bender listened to me ponder possibilities, they had no advice whatsoever. It was the risk of travel up and down Hudson Road that tipped the scale.

Andy volunteered to keep an eye on the Bell homestead as he had often before. The place would run itself in my absence. So I fired up searches on the Internet to find and reserve accommodations where Hobo and I would be welcome. Hobo and I ended up on the Gulf coast of Florida near Vero Beach in a resort that featured comfortable casual cottages. Hobo adapted quickly to beach living. He loved his off-duty hours when he could splash in the water while I basked on a big towel on the sand. Otherwise my well-being in the house and on walks remained subject to his vigilance. We often stopped at Beanies, a sidewalk café, for a snack and a bottle of water; it was there I met the Willards, Canadian "snowbirds."

Tom Willard was a former railroad executive, loving retirement and endless fishing; his daughter-in-law Eva was recently a widow and fighting depression. He was about seventy, often out with his cronies on a boat, rod in hand. Eva was my age and lonesome. They had an overweight elderly golden retriever named Princess that Eva walked faithfully morning and afternoon. They also stopped at Beanies and Hobo and Princess struck up an easy friendship which led, of course, to acquaintance between me and Eva. Telling me her life story seemed therapeutic for Eva, so I listened at length, hoping God was giving me credit for a good deed. Eva was red-headed, very attractive, a beach bombshell in a bikini but usually shrouded in caftan to protect her fair skin from sunburn. I reciprocated with a carefully edited biography of my own. Any number of tanned, bleached-blond beach bums cruised past Beanies in the late afternoon attempting hits on Eva and me. I knew why I rejected their interest (I thought them vapid and only out for a dinner invitation followed by a quick lay) but I was puzzled by her indifference. Nevertheless she and I killed a lot of time with one another in what I'm sure she considered a friendship. I was OK with the acquaintance but rather leery of an intimacy. Many of Eva and Tom's questions dwelt on where and how I lived in Indiana.

Tom, Eva, and I, accompanied by our canines, had Christmas dinner together at the Chateau de la Mer, an upscale restaurant on a rickety (I thought) pier. White-haired customers, many arriving with walkers or in wheelchairs, occupied most of the tables. Lobster and red snapper vied with turkey and roast beef on a bountiful buffet. The food was quite good but the crowd's holiday spirit was big on bottled holiday spirits and the ambience grew perceptibly rowdy after the buffet closed. I was witness for the first and only time in my life to a geriatric food fight. Tom stayed on, for the fun he said, but Eva and I escaped with the dogs to put up our feet on the lanai of my cottage. Drinks on top of antidepressant medication had brought Eva to an unusual degree of cheerful loquacity and she talked about a returning to Toronto to attend the wedding of Tom's stepdaughter on Valentine's Day. She prattled on about driving north through Indiana and visiting my home on the way. My evasions had given her an image of a rustic cabin in scenic surroundings of woods and watercourses, swarming with wild birds, deer, foxes, squirrels, possums, *et cetera*. "We wouldn't stay longer than overnight and Tom and I will take you out to eat. We wouldn't be any bother, I promise. I'm dying to see what it's like in southern Indiana where that beautiful limestone comes from."

My antennae were picking up danger signals. I plied Eva with Cherry Heering, calling it a nightcap, until she stumbled home ready for bedtime. When I was sure she and Tom were both out of the way, I called Ben Bender's 24/7 number, told his answering machine the story of my day, and urged a reply as soon as feasible. On the 28th, O'Leary called and told me to go off to as private a place as I could find and call him back. I put Hobo in the car and drove to an overlook in the Everglades where alligators and anhingas were the only eavesdroppers on my conversation.

O'Leary tried to sound upbeat but I could tell he was worried.

"I checked out the Willards and they are who they say they are. But Tom Willard failed to mention that he's a mechanical engineer and sits on the board of The Hankins Company. His stepdaughter is marrying one of Clyde's nephews. I think Tom and Eva aim to weasel their way into the house on Bald Knob to assess your Cousin Willy's defense system. I talked to Andy van Houten and he told me there has been no sign of intruders around the house or in Corona. The Patriot Guard is still putting out feelers in the area but has been stymied by the task force's surveillance."

Apologetically I told him, "I've tried to be cagey and keep specifics out of my conversations with Tom and Eva. I've never mentioned Corona. When I had to say something about my home, I focused on its remoteness and difficulty of access. I'm not good at lying and I may have let slip more than I intended. What do you advise?"

"Drop the Willards as soon as you can without tipping them off to your uneasiness. Maybe a stealthy exit from the resort without leaving a forwarding address will do it. I don't advise a return to Bald Knob until better weather up there. Andy told me there's been an unusual amount of frost heave on Hudson Road this year and the county has posted it as impassable.

"OK," I said. "I'll do something to shed them and their interest in my business. You'll hear from me as soon as I get free."

My chance came when one of Tom's pals invited him and Eva to a New Year's Eve bash at his year-round house in Vero Beach. They urged me to come along but I said no, I wouldn't know anybody, and wasn't that keen on drinking in the New Year. After they left for the party, I left a note on their door, Family Emergency! then packed up and Hobo and I hit the road. We ended up two days later in Atlanta and I sent word to the management of the resort that I wouldn't be back. I assured them of my satisfaction with my stay, refused a refund on the rental, and asked them not to give out my home address or phone number. The amount of the refund was substantial and I counted on that to bribe their discretion.

I would have enjoyed the next month thoroughly in Atlanta if I hadn't felt like a felon on the run. B.O.&S. approved and Ben Bender urged me to sample the highlights of the town—his undergraduate and graduate studies at Emory University had given him boundless affection for the area. None of the activities I would have enjoyed, such as Philharmonic concerts, dramatic productions, and the Museum, allowed pets and Hobo wasn't happy in his crate in the motel. Every time I prepared to leave him, his downcast attitude made me feel guilty. We walked a lot but the parks weren't that much fun in the winter season. Somehow O'Leary had learned that the Willards' choice of the resort had been suggested by Clyde Hankins *after* I had arrived there. That really made me mad. I resented being hounded by Hankins and feared he might try similar tricks on any of my vacations from the Bell homestead.

I couldn't wait to get back to Bald Knob but Andy said falling rocks had blocked Hudson Road and the county couldn't clear it until April at the earliest. The only way to the Bell homestead for Hobo and me would be by way of Andy's road and his ATV path. By the middle of February I was so sick of being homeless, I drove to Corona and parked my Jeep at Andy's cottage. Hobo and I hiked to our place while Andy transported our luggage on the ATV. We arrived, somewhat footsore, to the warmth and comfort of the big living room and a meal of pork and beans from the pantry. I willingly lived out of the pantry and freezer with occasional supplements of fresh vegetables (courtesy of Andy's shopping) until the middle of April. By the time I made the trip to Nell's living room, I was *very* shaggy, but I wasn't about to expend the energy needed to walk Eugenia's trail or to my car at Andy's house just to get a haircut.

Spring came to Bald Knob with a bang in May and Hobo and I checked out all our favorite trails. The trail to Eugenia's house passed through the remnants of an old apple orchard in blossom. Bees hummed busily and delicate color and sweet odors filled the air. The weather had provided Cassie with so much small prey that she had no time to lurk in ambush and Hobo passed unchallenged. Eugenia's house and barn were almost lost in fresh foliage and lingering wild plum and dogwood flowers. I found her on her knees digging up the sandy loam of her vegetable garden. She dusted off her hands and invited me to the porch for sassafras tea.

"Stop making those faces," she ordered. "It's spring tonic, good for you."

I wasn't convinced but after several determined gulps, I decided I could finish my serving. Eugenia went back to putting in the tomato and pepper plants she had started from seed on a sunny windowsill inside the house. "My, won't them tomatoes taste good in a month or so." She licked her lips and my salivary glands agreed with her. In the course of our conversation, she told me of an encounter she had had in January with three Patriot Guardsmen, toting rifles and prowling the lower reaches of her land. At the time she was on her way to Corona with a burlap bag full of bowls she intended to put on sale in Burr Worman's store.

"They acted like I was the trespasser. I spoke to 'em pretty firm and got a blast of cuss words in reply but they turned around and headed back toward the road. I took a side trail to Corona so I wouldn't run into them again. Got to Burr's store and found their pickup parked there. They came in and gave Burr a hard time while I was there. Had him scared. When they left, I gave Burr a lecture and made him call the task force number. He didn't want to, 'fraid they'd come back to do him harm, but I insisted. That Deputy Roth came on foot up Hudson Road to see me and ask questions. I told her I looked 'em over pretty good and my descriptions were accurate. I liked her. Smart and pretty too."

"Eugenia, do you have a phone? If you don't…"

She looked rather sheepish. "Yes, a while back Willy had a line run. He said he was paying for the service. Said I needed a way to tell him or Andy or even Burr if I got sick or hurt. He even put the numbers in for me. I was embarrassed. All these years I got along just dependin' on myself, didn't think I needed anyone ever to help, hated to accept it but he meant well. I didn't want to look a gift horse in the mouth. But, you know, I'm so used to doing without it, I usually don't remember I got it."

Before Hobo and I started for home, I asked to see the phone and get the number. I decided I'd call her some of the times I didn't come over. Maybe getting a call now and then would reconcile her to calling out when she needed to. After my experience with false friends, I didn't intend to risk losing one I prized.

Having been reminded of my obligations to true friends, I invited Andy for a special dinner: roast beef, mashed potatoes and gravy, peas, carrots, home-baked rolls, chocolate cake. After his second wedge of cake, he sighed in repletion and leaned back in his chair.

"You're a swell cook. If I thought you wouldn't be insulted, I'd ask you to marry me."

I appreciated his comment but I had an answer. "I'd be honored, but I wouldn't accept your offer. I've decided I'm a loner, pleased with a friend like you but not ready to consider long-term commitments. Now, are *you* insulted?"

"Heck, no. I'm glad you are so honest. Let's just leave it that you're the kind of girl I'd like to marry. You know, as I look back on trying to make a life with Gerda, I realize how foolish I was and how smart she was. We weren't right for one another, didn't really know one another, didn't share any dreams. She hated it here, couldn't wait to leave. I felt rejected but I should have felt relieved that she broke it off. Now, since you cooked, I'll clear the table and load the dishwasher."

After Andy had gone home and I was curled up in front of the embers of the fireplace, I thought about being a loner. Had it always been my destiny or had I made it so? A lot of women my age were dating handsome, well-mannered men and a lot of them were marrying the steady hard-working ones and having babies. But I wasn't like a lot of women. Besides Andy was the only male to frequent Bald Knob, and although he fitted the picture—good-looking, cultivated, reliable, hard-working—it was his *friendship* I prized. I had not ever felt lonely on Bald Knob, I was usually too busy. As I thought more about being alone, I drifted off to sleep with

Hobo's head in my lab. As matters were to develop, being a loner became gratuitous.

The next day, one of those June days of which poets sing, Eugenia came for a soup-and-sandwich lunch. After she left I felt restless and decided to wash my car. The county's fix of Hudson Road had consisted in large measure of dumping clay on the berms and tamping it down. When the weather was dry, the clay made dust; when it was wet, it made mud. Whatever it made collected on my Jeep until the yellow stripes were indistinguishable from the red background. I put on boots, raggedy jeans, and a shirt that had seen better days and set to work with hose, soap, and old washcloths. Hobo supervised from the veranda; he loved water but hated the mud puddle I made. His single sharp bark alerted me to the crunch of gravel in the lane and a white Prius nosing into the parking area. He left the veranda, skirted the puddle on dainty feet, and stood on alert as the driver stopped and lowered the window. I twisted the nozzle of the hose to shut off the water and stepped over to the car. The driver was a woman in her 30s with a chic haircut and artfully applied makeup.

"Miss Bell, I hope I may have a few minutes of your time. I tried to call but could find no number for you. Is it safe to get out of the car?"

"Do you have a business card?" I asked.

She fumbled in her purse and handed a card out to me. I read it and stuck it in my shirt pocket. It identified her as Henrietta McNee, Realtor, Commercial Properties, and listed an address and phone number in Greenwood.

"Hobo, sit, stay! You can get out, Ms. McNee, if you like. Watch your feet. The ground is pretty muddy. What is your business here?"

She eased out of the car, one eye on Hobo, and I suddenly became aware of my bedraggled appearance. Muddy boots, shirt and jeans wet and smeared with dirt, were a marked antithesis to her smartly tailored, pale-green linen pants suit. She reached out for a handshake but when I backed off, showing my muddy fingers, she got down to business.

"I represent a real estate developer in search of a large tract with potential for development. He is looking to buy 200 acres of Bell land and splitting it into six to eight scenic building sites for luxury vacation homes selling for one to two million dollars each. I've been asked to scout the land and assess the possibilities. I've researched the public documents in the offices of the county clerk and surveyor and learned that the land is owned by a trust administered by Dennis O'Leary of the firm of Bocce, O'Leary, and Shapiro."

"I have not been informed that Bell property is up for sale." My response was cool.

"Ah, yes. I understand that you, Miss Rebecca Bell, are only the current tenant and caretaker. My negotiations on behalf of my client will be with Mr. O'Leary. I'm hoping you will allow me to walk around easily accessible areas of the land and to evaluate the rather eclectic building I see here for possible use as the developer's offices."

"You seem to be well-informed. However, I am not authorized to allow random visitors to the property. You may leave now. Please contact Mr. O'Leary at your earliest convenience." I was rather proud of my calm, cool delivery of businesslike jargon. Ms. McNee was not one to give up easily.

"I am also instructed to contact a Mrs. Baker whose land abuts this. I understand her residence is located at the dead end of Hudson Road. How much farther is that from the Bell lane?"

Unholy glee almost overwhelmed my cool demeanor. "About three quarters of a mile past the Bell mailbox. However, the county has declared that segment of Hudson Road impassable to vehicular traffic. You will have to walk."

Ms. McNee's face fell in disappointment but then assumed a look of alarm as she turned to open her car door. She found herself obliged to scuttle to get the car door open and herself inside. I had opened the nozzle on the hose and the pent-up pressure kicked up a little fountain of mud that splattered the front fender of the car. Though not intentional, that served as a dismissal. Her goodbye, delivered through the open window, was polite but chilly.

I finished my job. Hobo returned to the veranda and resumed his snooze. My mind was turning over possibilities very different from those Ms. McNee hoped to consider. Were her inquiries legitimate? It would be a bold, even reckless, developer who saw potential for million dollar houses on Bell or Baker land. Or was she perhaps a front? Maybe for The Patriot Guard or Clyde Hankins? Her allusion to the building seemed to imply a new ploy by Hankins to gain access to Cousin Willy's workrooms.

I finished up with the car, stowed the equipment, and went indoors for a bath and fresh clothes. It was only 3:30 so I called Ben Bender with a report of Ms. McNee's visit. After recording my tale, he drawled a comment, "Something new every day. I'll save this one for Dan tomorrow morning." O'Leary had left the office early for an event at his grandson's school. I didn't lose any sleep over this encounter. I hadn't sensed any threat in Ms. McNee's visit. However, I called Andy to set up a shooting lesson. At the last one I had killed the oak tree six times and inflicted flesh wounds the other four times. I wasn't flinching when I fired. I wasn't feeling belligerent. Nevertheless, I believed in honoring the Scout motto: Be prepared! as well as that other old saw: Practice makes perfect!

O'Leary called back the next afternoon. After complimenting me on handling another situation well, he told me he had engaged a PI to look into Ms. McNee's connections. "Her story looks innocent on the surface but any developer stands in dire need of a sanity check if he is real and really wants to develop housing on the Bell and Baker lands. It would be nice, wouldn't it, if you didn't have to deal with any more of these weird cases?"

I agreed but didn't tell him how grateful I was that none of them had had unhappy outcomes—so far, that is.

A few days after the last unwelcome visit, Hobo and I walked a trail that took us within 200 or so yards of the Corona road. My hiking wardrobe had expanded beyond binoculars and now included the cell phone in my pocket and a holstered water bottle on my belt. At the extremity of the trail I stopped for a quick quaff while Hobo roamed the underbrush. Suddenly he was standing in front of me with a wet, cold, dirty, *furry* thing in his mouth. "If that's a rat," I scolded, "you can just put it back where you found it." Instead he dropped the thing at my feet. When it stirred feebly and mewed faintly, I saw it was a kitten someone had dumped on the roadside to die. It was quite young but its eyes were already open. It looked to be in bad shape but when I picked it up and held it to my chest, a faint purr plucked at my heartstrings. I started for the house as fast as I could go, Hobo beside me.

At the house a bout of furious activity ensued. I microwaved a hand towel and wrapped the kitten in its warmth. I looked for bloody wounds in case of injuries by an unsuccessful predator but found none. I held the cat's nose to warm milk in a saucer but got no response. I remembered that my bottle of red food coloring had come with a dropper and I dug it out of the cupboard. Prying the cat's mouth open, I dribbled milk into it until the kitten began to swallow. That the milk was pink didn't seem a problem. I kept up with the milk until the kitten fell asleep with a distended belly. Not until then did I stop to draw breath and consider further action.

I went down to the basement, brought up a laundry basket, and made a nest of another towel. I knew that sooner or later I would have to make provision for the cat to eliminate. So I cut the side out of an empty cereal box, filled it with shredded newspaper, and put it into the basket next to the nest. I blessed my luck when the kitten woke up, nosed the impromptu litter box, and used it. Apparently it had spent enough time with its mother to have learned basic feline manners. Handling the kitten I had discovered it was female. "She may not live," I told Hobo, who had watched my every move and now sat on guard beside the basket. "But she needs a name. What do you think of She? She-Ba? Sheba?" Hobo approved with a soft woof.

I spent the next 18 hours dribbling warm milk into Sheba every few hours. The next morning she was staggering around the basket quite briskly but I nevertheless had her in the basket at the door of Hobo's vet in Greenwood when it opened. I wasn't about to let the beast die and my sleepless night go to waste. Dr. Mac is not impressive at first glance; he's sort of wimpy-looking, short, skinny, with strands of pale hair slicked down over an advanced case of male pattern baldness, but he has the kindest hands and eyes of anyone I've ever known. He gave Sheba a thorough examination and me an optimistic report.

"She needs a bath and treatment for fleas. Her heart is strong but her lungs are congested. Eyes are affected by the respiratory infection, gummy but not permanently damaged. She's about five weeks old and very thin but your treatment has her well-hydrated and she'll live. What are you going to do with her? Keep or shelter?"

I looked at Hobo and he looked back with "keep" in his eyes. He seemed to be reminding me of the Chinese axiom: save a life and you are eternally responsible for it. I told Dr. Mac we would be adopting Sheba. He suggested leaving her with him for a couple of days while he loaded her up with antibiotics and immunizations.

"When you and Hobo come back for her, we'll do the paper work and chip her. Then you can go to the pet store over on Main Street and invest in equipment for cat care. Take this pamphlet and read up on your new pet." And that's the way it worked out. Sheba was clean, sweet-smelling, and purring when we left the clinic with orders to return in 8 weeks for spaying. She proved to have a thick, mostly white coat, with a black saddle, mask, and mustache. As her health returned, her eyes bloomed in her face like green lanterns.

Sheba seemed to want to follow Hobo's routine of mealtimes and sleep. All I had to do was make allowances for the difference in their ages, diets, and temperaments. She did not so much fit into our routines as we adapted to hers. I managed to teach her to stay off the tables and counters but I had to have her front claws removed in order to save Cousin Willy's expensive upholstered furniture. The inconveniences she caused us were more than compensated by the affection and entertainment she gave in return. Hobo watched over her like a doting nanny. I suspected that he stretched out deliberately to make a warm cradle between his front legs. Andy fell in love with her. She was cuddled in his lap one evening after she had exhausted herself in wild play when I wondered aloud what we would do with her if Hobo and I escaped to sunny climes next winter. "Why, of course, she'll come to stay with *me!*" he said. The emphasis was unmistakable.

Eugenia laughed at Hobo, Andy, and me. "I didn't expect you'd ever have a cat but as soon as you did, I was sure you make yourselves fools over it. Cassie came to me the same way Sheba came to you. Found her on the roadside with a broken leg, took her in and patched her up, babied her ever since. She's a great comfort on chilly nights, sleeps on my feet. She can embarrass me, bit the young fella that put in the telephone, unprovoked. She just likes to let folks know who's boss."

In August Eugenia fell out of an apple tree and broke a leg. She crawled to the house and called me. "I'm pretty sure I can't handle this by myself. The bone is sticking out of the flesh. What do you think?"

My thinking was to call Greenwood Emergency Services and request immediate dispatch. They told me it would take 90 minutes to get to our location, so I rushed over to her house, wrapped her wound in clean linen, gave her two aspirins and a lecture, and put the teakettle on for a hot drink. She lay stretched out on a rug on the floor, gritting her teeth and all the while telling me she was OK, that I should let her wait alone for the EMS people. I had to tell her in no uncertain terms that I was in charge, that I had explained the problems of access to EMS and they had assured me they were accustomed to handling emergencies in difficult, remote locations. I arranged for them to call her number as they started up Hudson Road for the Bell lane, *then* I would leave for the Bell house to guide them to hers. I met the ambulance as it drove into my parking area. Two husky young men and an emergency technician took out a collapsible litter and two big bags of equipment and followed me down the secret trail, secret no longer, to the Baker house. I decided I was in better shape than they were; they were huffing and puffing when we got there but conditioned by walks with

Hobo, I hadn't turned a hair. I was amused that Eugenia played gracious hostess on our arrival; she offered us all a drink of cold well water before we tended her. But the techs set out immediately to checking vital signs and the wound and preparing her for the trip to the hospital.

Cassie watched everything from a vantage point under a bureau. I assured Eugenia I would look after the cat until she got back. "You won't have to," she said. "She's like me, able to look after herself, but thanks for the offer. Willy made me sign up for Medicare a few years back. The important paper is in that top drawer of the bureau. My purse with some cash is on the bedside stand."

The EMS people soon had her ready to go. Trailed by Hobo and me, they carefully negotiated the difficult footing of the twisting, narrow trail to Bald Knob. At the ambulance Eugenia was transferred from the litter to a gurney. The process caused her to faint but she roused long enough to hear me tell her I was following in the car to be with her at Greenwood Medical Center. I hastily locked the Bell house and called Andy to bring him up to date. Then Hobo and I took off for Greenwood. We rolled into parking at the emergency entrance right after the ambulance.

Since there was no one else to assume the role, I became Eugenia's "responsible party." The paper work didn't take long, she was whisked away to surgery, and I was exiled to the surgical waiting room. It was a dreary, wearisome, worrisome wait. The reading material consisted of antique Reader's Digests and week-old newspapers; the room was shabby and smelled of stale, sour smoke deposited on fabrics prior to contemporary no-smoking regulations; the temperature was 80 degrees and there was no way to open a window. On two occasions a nurse or aide poked a head through a barely open door and skittered off before I could ask for news. Hobo was shut up in the car in the parking area with windows cracked open an inch. I was so bored and tired I almost *wanted* an SPCA officer to hunt me up and cite me for animal cruelty. I paced, then sat, then paced some more. In the fifth hour, a young doctor in a white coat appeared. Embroidered on his breast pocket was the name Thomas Grant, M.D.

"Are you Mrs. Baker's granddaughter? I have good news for you."

"I'm Rebecca Bell, Mrs. Baker's neighbor. Tell me, I've been so worried."

"Ms. Bell, Mrs. Baker has a compound fracture of the fibula. We have reduced it and placed pins. If there are no complications, she should make a complete recovery in six to eight weeks. She was lucky. I understand she fell out of a tree—what she was doing in a tree at her age is a mystery—a fractured tibia would have been much more serious, high risks for pulmonary embolism. I was told she lives alone. She must stay in hospital care for at least a week, thereafter in assisted living until she is fully mobile again. Since she identified no next of kin, I will turn her case over to Eldercare Services…"

"No. No. No need for that. I will take complete responsibility for her until she can be on her own. If need be, I can arrange fulltime nursing care in my home. May I see her now?"

"She's in the recovery room and will stay there for several more hours. You may see her for fifteen minutes and then I suggest you come back tomorrow morning. She will be under heavy sedation until then."

Eugenia looked very small and fragile, her hair on the pillow as white as the fabric, the tan on her face faded to a bleak yellow color. But she responded to my voice with a whisper and a weak smile. "Becca! Thank you for looking after me. I'm very sleepy but the doctor told me I would be OK and that you were going to make sure."

"Yes, don't worry about anything. He thought I was your granddaughter and I'm going to pretend I am until you are on your feet again. Now you rest and I'll see you in the morning. OK?"

Her lips formed an OK as her lids were closing. I patted her hand and slipped out of the room, tears stinging my eyes. Hobo was glad to see me and since he had been cooped up for almost 6 hours, I let him out in the city park briefly and bought him and me ice cream cones from the concessionaire. A lonesome Sheba welcomed us home with loud squalls I interpreted as pleasure.

I was beginning to realize the extent of my hasty commitment to Eugenia's immediate future. I needed to talk it over with someone so I called Andy and invited him to supper. I had stopped at the supermarket in Greenwood and purchased deli coleslaw, baked beans, buns, and fresh-ground hamburger. As we ate I filled Andy in on Eugenia's condition and my decision to look after her.

"You and Hobo are quite the Samaritans, aren't you? First Sheba and now Eugenia. I think you are doing the right thing but it may not be as easy as you thought when you made your promises. What can I do to help?"

"Just talk out my doubts with me, please. My promises mean that Hobo and I won't be escaping to sunny climes this winter. Staying here with an invalid guest creates some problems. My bank balance can afford to pay a nurse to look after Eugenia in the short-term but I won't be able to keep house, cook, do laundry, and look after her for a longer time. I'll need a house helper, probably for weeks. Give me some ideas how I can explain things to O'Leary. He said the trust could pay for household staff but that was when I was sole occupant. Other people in the house raises questions about the access to Bald Knob in bad weather, hauling in groceries and supplies, nurse and helper coming and going...."

"Let's start with access. Start with praying for a mild winter. Then have a plan for a bad one. Dress the Jeep in studded tires or have chains put on. That will get *you* in and out 95% of the time. If you stipulate live-in people for care-givers, you could chauffeur them from time to time. There are plenty of beds in this house, aren't there? If you get snowed in, which is unlikely, there's the ATV path and access to the outside from my house."

"What if Eugenia should need a doctor or EMS transport?"

"Don't forget I could ferry a doctor across the ridge from my house. EMS is prepared for trips in bad weather. No problem that I can see."

"Of course, but what about accommodating Eugenia here in the house? She won't be able to use stairs for weeks. I suppose we could bring a bed downstairs to the sitting room that's next to the powder room. The powder room could be used for bed-baths and bedpans."

"Rather than lugging a bed down here, I think it would make better sense to rent a hospital bed. More comfortable for her and handier for a nurse or helper. There's a medical supply company in Greenwood that would advise on the best kind and deliver it. And a wheelchair when she's no longer bedfast."

"Oh, Andy! I love your good advice! You are so helpful. All the things I haven't thought out...." I jumped up and threw my arms around him. Sheba, dislodged from his lap, let out a yell of displeasure. I had learned that she was far more prompt and vocal than Hobo to communicate her feelings. I sat down again and we began to consider some details.

When I called O'Leary the next morning, I had a fairly complete picture of ways to handle an invalid in the house. He said the wording of the trust specifically covered household help and was without restrictions. If the nurse and expenditures for care of a guest were my personal expense, he saw no difficulty other than the amount I was willing to spend. He laughed when I told him my bank balance was bulletproof until the bills for a full length chinchilla coat and twenty carat diamond ring came due. Ben Bender was instructed to work up a list of employment agencies that offered suitable personnel and to add a helper's salary to the household expense ledger as soon as I engaged one. Best wishes for Eugenia's rapid recovery concluded my conversations with the B.O.&S offices.

When I arrived with a pot of scarlet asters later in the day, I found Eugenia perky but fretting. "Food's terrible and they keep waking me up all night to ask if I'm sleeping well!" I had a conference with Dr. Grant and came away with a list of do's and don'ts and recommendations for carrying out my plans at Bald Knob.

Everything came together nicely. Eugenia came to the Bell homestead on the 13th day after her accident and settled in comfortably. Mary Cadwell, the nurse sent by the agency, had had a lot of experience with compound fractures. She was delighted with her luxurious bedroom on the second floor, complimented me profusely on my cooking, and groaned every time travel on Hudson Road was mentioned. She was also dismayed by Sheba's incorrigible penchant to be Eugenia's roommate and frequent bedmate. Hobo was in dismay because he was forbidden to attend Sheba in Eugenia's room until her wound had closed.

The helper arrived the day before Mary left. Her name was Felicity Rosenbaum. She was almost as tall as I, robust, almost obese, hair clipped to half-inch length, big expressive brown eyes. She tackled every job with a song on her lips and unquenchable enthusiasm. I had chosen her, sight unseen, from among three contenders. She had glowing references and a résumé filled out in conventional style, but it was the brief essay she appended that won my heart.

> "Born in Alabama, as a young girl went to New York City for a job. Married to Israel Rosenbaum, a tailor, for 35 years. When he passed, took jobs as a live-in helper all over the country just for the adventure of it. People call me Rosy which is fun since I am just about as black as a black person can get. My hobby is needlepoint. I must have a TV set in my room. I can cook kosher if that should be wanted."

I judged she would be an unusual and grateful addition to our diverse household. Her first words on arrival informed me that the trip up Hudson Road had almost turned her white and she wasn't going to brave a trip down very soon, if ever. She appeared for her first work day in a black, long-sleeved shirtwaist dress, calf-length, with black hose and shoes. A demure white collar and a sizable white apron completed the look. She reacted to the surprise on my face with an apology.

"I'm sorry, ma'am. I have white uniforms upstairs. I'll go change…."

"Oh, no, no, no," I hastened to say. "I didn't want a servant. I need a helper, someone to help with the laundry, cooking, and housekeeping. There's no formality here at Bald Knob. Please wear everyday, ordinary clothes and *don't* call me ma'am. Call me Rebecca or Becca as you choose."

Now a big smile replaced the surprise on *her* face as I continued. "Get changed into comfortable clothes. I planned to give the kitchen a thorough cleaning today and you'll need to get acquainted with Eugenia. OK?"

She and Eugenia hit it off right away. Within a week Rosy was teaching Eugenia needlepoint.

The day after Rosy's arrival, Eugenia asked me to go over to her house and bring back a few of her things. So Hobo and I made the Bell-Baker trail our walk that afternoon. The weather was crisp and clear; a mild frost had started to turn a few leaves to red and gold; squirrels were hurrying to stow away their winter food. We had a surprise when Cassie met us at the boundary of her domain, her attitude ingratiating, her tail a flag of truce instead a proclamation of combat. Although Hobo remained wary, he relaxed somewhat. When we reached the Baker clearing, I first scouted the vegetable garden and barn. The kiln was cold, the products of the last firing stacked neatly on shelves in the barn. Vegetables above ground had been ravaged, probably by deer or raccoons, and Eugenia's shovel lay by a dug-up patch of dirt, starting to rust. Odd, I thought, she always puts away the tools from the last task before starting the next one. I stowed the shovel in the barn and went to the house. I had tidied its minor clutter and closed all the doors and windows before I left to follow the EMS crew. But entering now I realized things weren't right. The pantry door stood ajar and cans lay in a jumble on the floor. Kitchen drawers and cabinets had been opened, dishes and pans taken out and piled on the floor. In the bedroom the mattress was pulled half off the bed and bureau drawers were pulled out, their contents disturbed. Someone (a burglar?) had rummaged the place. I remembered a small wooden box Eugenia had once taken from a drawer to show me old-fashioned gold jewelry that had been her mother's.

When I looked through the drawers for the things I had been sent to bring back, the box was gone. The pattern of disorder made me think the intruder had been looking for cash and valuables. As I gathered stuff—comb, brush, some underwear, two dresses, and a smock—into a basket, I was careful not to touch any more surfaces than I had to. Eugenia had also told me where to find her grandfather's cane. She planned to use it soon! While I worked, Cassie wove herself between and around my legs, purring mightily. I dared not touch her but she looked good; she wasn't skinny, her coat was glossy, she had no scars. She was interested in the cat treats I put down on the porch but didn't gobble them as if starved. I would have a good report of Cassie to take to Eugenia but I had already made up my mind to keep her in the dark about the "burglary."

I closed up the house again and took out my cell phone to call Special Deputy Roth. I had to leave voice mail but I knew I would hear from her soon. I started back on the Bell-Baker trail. "Trail" was a misnomer, it was not an footpath in the ordinary sense of the word. It consisted of a series of landmarks that Eugenia had taught me—limestone outcrops and ledges; oddly shaped boulders; lightning-blasted stumps; fallen trees. I wouldn't be able to follow the landmarks point to point in the dark but I had them down pat by day. The question that bothered me was whether the burglar had used the trail to reach Eugenia's house. I had guided the EMS crew to the Baker house and back using those landmarks but I was sure the crew was not memorizing them for future use; those folks were too concerned with their footing and managing their equipment and the litter. I eventually concluded the secret trail was still secret. The burglar could only have reached the Baker clearing on foot through the forest or across the tumbled slabs and scree of the section of Hudson Road that the county and the post office deemed impassable.

Deputy Roth returned my call before Hobo and I had got back to Bald Knob. I told her of my findings and suspicions. When I said I had tried to leave things as much undisturbed as I could, she was pleased. Fingerprints! Missing jewelry had a way of turning up! She wasn't convinced it was a Patriot Guard job but there had been another report of pilfering from an unoccupied home located along the Corona road. She would be investigating and interviewing Eugenia for an exact description of the jewelry. I begged her not to approach Eugenia too soon. I kept reminding her Eugenia was old, injured, and shouldn't be stressed by knowing her home had been violated. Grudgingly Deputy Roth promised to put off the interview until after the fingerprints had been obtained and identified, maybe for another week. I had to accept that.

I found Rosy in a rocking chair on the veranda with a cup of coffee in her hand. "Got my work done and Genie's napping. You look hot and tired. Come sit down a little. Can I get you coffee or a cold drink?"

I accepted the offer of a glass of ice water and flopped in another rocking chair. When Rosy returned with the water, she entered on a paean of praise for the lavish comfort of her accommodations. "I never had such a grand place, not even when I worked for that star in Hollywood. I won't mention her name but the house was a ten-million-dollar wonder and I was allowed to use the pool in the early morning. But the spa tub here is even better; warm water in motion is great for hard-working muscles. This house has as many bedrooms as hers does. Say, I put together a nice casserole with the leftover chicken and some broccoli that I found in the freezer and some rice and it'll be real nice for supper. Do you mind? Your cooking is good but I had time and Genie thought she might like to come to the table in her wheel chair."

I congratulated myself on picking Rosy as an addition to our household. Her good humor and immense fund of pleasant conversation made good company for Eugenia. I had been concerned that she was growing depressed with her shut-in status, and afraid that boredom would have her trying out her grandfather's cane too soon. I didn't think she could get even a little bit bored with Rosy around. The casserole was delicious and dinner was a happy event with Eugenia laughing and telling stories of her youth to entertain Rosy and me. Andy also approved of Rosy as he got to know her over the next week or so. Approved and more because she made Krumkakke (as she called it although Mary Conrad would have called it crumb cake) which Andreas loved because his grandmother used to make it when he was a child.

Deputy Roth waited the promised week before interviewing Eugenia for a description of the jewelry. By that time the fingerprint analysis was back and two individuals had been identified as the burglars. Both had records for minor felonies and both were thought to be Patriot Guardsmen. Eugenia's reaction to the burglary was outrage. Red-faced in her indignation, she ranted.

"Deputy, I'm pressing charges against those bastards. I want you to fill out the papers to get it done. I've lived more than 80 years on that land, and my forebears lived on it for nigh 200 years before me. No one has a right to come on it and take what is mine. I've got my will made out and all 800 acres of that land is going to the State to be a park and nature preserve. I'm the only one left of the Millmans and Bakers and it's up to me to preserve it. I won't have one inch of it sullied by the feet of this renegade bunch that thinks they got to save the country by fostering hate and dissension. If I had 'em here I'd use this cane to teach them a lesson. My granddaddy carved it out of an oaken tree limb and did the blacksmithin' to set the iron on the end of it." In her anger she thumped her granddaddy's cane on the Bell family's floor planks hard enough to make dents.

I had grown alarmed for Eugenia's blood pressure as she ranted on, but the more she got off her chest, the better she seemed to feel. When she finally ran down, her eyes were bright, her color was good, and her voice was strong. The will to fight had routed the tendency to depression that had worried me. Deputy Roth left with several pages of notes gleaned from her interview. Eugenia had made her promise to keep her informed of the task force's progress to find and bring the burglars to justice.

Things settled into an agreeable household routine. Eugenia was walking with the cane now and yearning to tackle the stairs for a bath in a tub. I caught her one day wistfully eying the stair. "I think I could make it. If I were to list my most earnest wishes, soaking in one of Willy's fancy tubs would be at the top!"

"Why?" I asked.

"I was married once for a little while and the only nice thing that no-good husband ever did for me was to take me to Kansas City on our honeymoon. The bathtub in the hotel had an unending amount of hot water. We never had anything like that at the Baker house," she sighed.

I gave her a hug and a promise. "Just wait. Rosy and I will give you a royal soak upstairs for Christmas."

Routine lasted until Rosy and Eugenia put their heads together on plans for a Thanksgiving Day bash.

Eugenia reminisced. "It's been many a year since I had family and friends around a bountiful table. Of course, there's no family left for me but you friends are family from now on. We owe ourselves a family dinner. With Andy we'll be four around the table and Hobo and Sheba beneath it."

Chilly weather had set in but clear skies persisted and Hudson Road stayed passable. I was dispatched to the Greenwood A&P with a grocery list as long as my arm. The Thanksgiving feast was everything magazine articles and TV shows prescribed: a turkey bulging with giblet and pecan stuffing according to Rosy's mother's recipe; mashed potatoes and gravy, sweet potatoes candied according to Eugenia's instructions (rum in the glaze!), English peas in cream sauce and green beans dotted with bacon chips; frozen cranberry dessert *a la* Mary Conrad; pumpkin pie and mincemeat tarts at Andy's request. As grace, Eugenia and Rosy sang a duet—the first verse of *We gather together to ask the Lord's blessing.* I had to withdraw briefly to wipe my eyes and blow my nose. I didn't feel at all apologetic for yielding to emotion. Hobo and Sheba were treated with white and dark turkey meat tastefully garnished with a bit of gravy. At my command, everybody, including the animals, repaired to the living room to nap while I loaded the dishwasher as penance for overindulgence. I fixed a paper plate of turkey scraps, grabbed Cousin Willy's sheepskin jacket, and headed for the Baker place. The exercise did me good and Cassie was delighted with her turkey treat. While I was over there I checked the house and barn. Other than fingerprint powder on every surface, everything was as I had left it the last time I had visited. I was tempted to remedy the disorder that was still in evidence but refrained until I had talked to Deputy Roth. The house might still be a crime scene.

Christmas came, celebrated by another feast and a tree in the living room, courtesy of Andy and his axe. Eugenia got the tub bath I had promised but Rosy and I were in agreement that she should still be limited to sleeping quarters on the first floor. A major snowfall in the second week of December, ruled out the lower reaches of Hudson Road for all but emergency travel. The white Christmas was nice but it also ruled out shopping trips. Of necessity and by common consent, all gifts were handmade or homegrown.

Andy surprised us with a crock of wild bee honey. He had spotted a bee tree in September and had braved its occupants to loot their golden treasure. We slathered it generously on the dinner rolls I had baked. Eugenia handed out needlepoint bookmarks with designs as unique and charming as those she put on her pots. She was childishly proud of the new craft she had learned from Rosy during her convalescence. Rosy had raided the kindling box for pine cones to construct miniature trees which she painted with flour paste to mimic snow. They made elegant and unusual table decorations all over the house. I had just learned how to use a program Mike the GEEK had given me as a graduation gift when we ended his tutelage. The program let me pull graphic art off the Internet that I could incorporate into greeting card format with a message in my own words. I printed cards bearing individualized greetings for everyone and placed a card at each person's table setting for the Christmas feast. Sheba and Hobo each received stuffed sock toys crafted in collaboration among Rosy, Eugenia, and me. Andy brought a fresh beef bone for Hobo and tuft of feathers on a string for Sheba.

An unexpected thaw cleared almost all of the snow on Hobo's and my hiking trails and by mid-January I undertook a visit to the Baker place. I was surprised when Cassie failed to meet us on the path. That worried me. Had she succumbed to a predator or had she starved or frozen to death? Another thing worried me even more; the soft earth in the clearing around the house was covered with the prints of heavy boots. More than one intruder had left the prints and they looked fresh. Muddy smears soiled the porch floor and threshold of the door. Inside there was more sign of intruders and of damage they had added to the earlier disorder.

Sheathing had been ripped from the inside walls of the main room and bedroom, disclosing scorched surfaces on the boards. Eugenia had told us that her rather ramshackle house had replaced a more substantial building destroyed in a fire when she was a young woman; that the present house had been erected hastily with lumber salvaged from the ruins of the former dwelling; and that cavities between the inner and outer walls often harbored squirrels and raccoons. Were the intruders vandalizing the walls to search for something hidden in the cavities? Money? Valuables? Important papers? Muddy tracks appeared in every one of the four rooms of the house, even those with the walls left intact. Had the intruders found what they sought or had they just got tired of tearing off boards? I remembered Eugenia kept several large pots with close-fitting wooden lids in the pantry for storage of flour, sugar, and other staples. All of the storage pots had been dumped out, and two of them smashed. The damage brought tears to my eyes. Repairing it would be simple and inexpensive, but seeing it would break Eugenia's heart. This was her home!

I took out my cell phone and called Deputy Roth. She listened patiently while I described the situation, asked a few questions, and said she and her partner would be coming to look for clues. The boot prints in the mud could be very useful. She agreed that Eugenia would be devastated to know what had gone on and suggested I keep silent until the task force had some information to share. That might ease Eugenia's distress a bit. Hobo had waited for me on the porch; Cousin Willy had trained him to be polite and to wait for an invitation to enter the Baker house. Besides he had always had Cassie to avoid. I wondered if I should tell Eugenia that Cassie had not appeared.

Hobo and I were homeward bound when Hobo barked an alert and nosed into a patch of underbrush. I pushed aside a tangle of branches and found Cassie, hunched into a ball, her fur filthy with blood and dirt. When I said her name, she mewed weakly and stretched out one paw toward me. I took off the heavy cardigan I was wearing and cautiously lifted her into its folds. As I handled her, she yowled as if in pain but thank goodness, she didn't bite. With her cradled in my arms I hurried as fast as I could toward home. Hobo stayed close; I think he knew this was an emergency.

Rosy met me at the door. "Is that Genie's cat? What's happened to it? It's a good thing she's taking a nap. What shall we do with it?"

"Let's take her upstairs. There's a first aid kit in my bathroom. Looking her over will be a messy proposition. We'll have to wash off blood and mud to see what's wrong. The way she acted when I picked her up I thought maybe something was broken."

Hobo had broken the rule and followed us upstairs to observe. I wondered whether he expected to nanny Cassie as he had Sheba. An examination insofar as I could make it revealed a long deep gash, obviously infected and leaking stinky bloody fluid, on Cassie's right side. Her right foreleg hung limp. I knew our pathetic little first aid kit wasn't adequate to deal with her hurt. This was a job for Dr. Mac. I wrapped her up in the sweater again, went downstairs, and had Rosy bring the wash basket to me for transport. We had to be very quiet to avoid waking Eugenia. I grabbed my purse, loaded the cat into the Cherokee, and Hobo and I took off for Greenwood Pet Clinic. I thanked my good luck that Hudson Road was reasonably clear and that I could make good time.

Sara, the vet tech, immediately assessed Cassie as an emergency. She told a fussy woman with an obese beagle waiting for its annual physical that the cat took priority. The woman swallowed a hissy fit but finally subsided and flounced grumbling out of the door. I knew Dr. Mac had never seen Cassie before, Eugenia did not patronize vets. But he dropped everything for an animal in pain. Tenderly he lifted Cassie to the examining table. She yowled but didn't resist the exam.

"This is a bad one, Becca. Where did you find her? She's been shot. The infection is two to three days old. The bullet entered high on the shoulder, chipped the bone, and proceeded to tear open the skin over the ribs until it lodged in a fold of skin. This leg is broken but not by the bullet. I suspect after she was shot, someone grabbed the leg, swung her around, and then threw her. I'm not optimistic about a recovery. What do you want me to do?"

"Do whatever you can to save her. She's the sole companion of a lonely old woman who lives at the head of Hudson Road."

"Eugenia Baker, the potter? My wife collects her work."

"Yes, she broke her leg in September and has been staying at my house to recuperate. Do you know her? She's something of a recluse."

"I don't, but my wife would climb mountains and swim rivers to get her pots. I guess you're telling me I should pull out all the stops to save the cat. All I can promise is to try. Leave her, basket and all, and I'll call you tomorrow to tell you how she's doing. OK?"

"Yes, but save the bullet if you can. There's a fair possibility it was one of those Patriot Guards who shot her. Deputy Roth will want the bullet for evidence."

I was sweeping leaves off the veranda the next morning when my cell phone rang. Dr. Mac was telling me Cassie had survived the night and the antibiotics were making headway against the infection. He had x-rayed her leg; the fracture was spiral and there was no hope of pinning it or placing a cast. He expected amputation would be required.

I gasped. "Cassie is almost feral, outdoors in all weathers. She's been surviving in good health on her own since Eugenia left home in September. She has an aggressive temperament and has terrorized Hobo. I was amazed that she didn't threaten to bite me or you. What kind of a life can she have three-legged?"

"Actually not bad, although she'll have to adapt to being an indoor cat. I won't amputate until the infection is controlled. She's not out of the woods yet. Call me tomorrow for news. If Mrs. Baker worries about a vet bill, tell her my wife will write it off for one of her blackware masterpieces."

Now I had a dilemma, two in fact: tell Eugenia about the wreck of her house; tell her about Cassie's injury. I decided for the time being to tell her nothing. It would be at least three months before she could take the Bell-Baker trail. Of course, in the meantime Rosy and I would have to entertain another houseguest, a three-legged feline that terrified my dog and might kill my cat. I sighed and relegated crossing that bridge until we were sure Cassie survived. Maybe her temper would improve with one less leg.

A month later I was bringing Cassie home to Bald Knob. Her wounds had healed and the hair on her shoulder and flank was beginning to grow back; she had been chipped, neutered, wormed, and immunized. Now she was growling like rolling thunder and glowering at Hobo and me through the wires of the carrying cage on the back seat next to two large bags of groceries from the A&P. Hobo sat gravely considering the situation from the passenger seat. I was carrying in groceries when Rosy met me at the door. She glanced at the car as she took the bags from me and said "Uh-oh." I brought in the cage and set it just inside the door of the big living room where Eugenia sat facing the fireplace with some needlework in her lap. I hung up my coat and took a seat opposite Eugenia's welcoming smile.

"Have a good trip? I hope you got some asparagus. I know a dandy way to prepare fresh spring asparagus."

"Yes," I said. "But I have to tell you something that may upset you."

"Well, get to it. You've been hiding that something from me for weeks and I'm tired of pretending I didn't notice." She laid her needlepoint on the coffee table and settled herself to listen.

I launched on the tale of the damage I found at her house four weeks ago and had now grown. "Beyond the earlier mess, there were muddy footprints all over, every cupboard and pantry door pulled open and contents dumped, every bureau drawer pawed through…even sheathing pulled off the inside walls. It looked as if the intruders were searching for something. Deputy Roth and her partner examined it all for fingerprints…."

In a voice softly but fiercely menacing, her face red with rage, her eyes glaring, Eugenia burst out, "Damn Patriot Guards, sons of Satan. They'll do anything to get me out of there. I don't mind the damage as much as I hate that they did it. That house isn't much but it's my own place!"

I recalled that she had said her cabin had replaced the more substantial building where she had lived as a young woman. When it burned, the present cabin had been thrown up hastily with lumber salvaged from the old house. The inside sheathing had been patched together from wainscoting and paneling.

"Do you think they might have found whatever was concealed in the cavity between the walls?" I asked.

Eugenia snorted, laughing as she answered, "Mouse turds, birds' nests, squirrels' nests, and welcome for the taking. I can get Burr Worman's son-in-law to repair the walls, he's handy with tools. I don't hide my valuables in the walls of my shack. But I'll have to show you my hiding place. I'll die someday and you'll have to find my will and the deed to the land. What else you got? I want to hear it all. Cassandra? Is she dead?"

"No, but she was gravely injured. I took her to the vet and she's well again." I went over to the carrier cage and pulled up the door. Cassie emerged like a bullet to cross the room and land in Eugenia's lap in a frenzy of mewing, yowling, purring, scrambling, wriggling, and cuddling. She had moved so fast that Eugenia hadn't noticed the absence of her right foreleg. Breathless from the onslaught and the effort of containing Cassie's frantic affection, Eugenia asked, "What's wrong with her? Has she gone crazy?"

"She's had a hard life since she last saw you. I think she's glad to be with you again." I then told the story of finding Cassie and taking her to Dr. Mac and his care of her over the past month.

When Eugenia sighed, "I'll never be able to pay that vet bill," I handed it to her. It was two pages, listing drugs, procedures, and kennel charges, but scrawled across the last page was "PAID IN FULL pending receipt of a Baker masterpiece, signed Dorothea Mac." Eugenia's tears smeared the ink a bit before she laid it on the coffee table beside her needlepoint.

Suddenly she squealed, "Where's her leg?" I told of the bullet that had wounded Cassie and would earn a Patriot Guard's sentence of three years in jail for cruelty to an animal. "Well deserved! If I were the judge, it would be thirty!" she said. In the end she had to wait for several months to counsel the judge handing out sentences to her burglars.

The first week of April Eugenia had proved herself able to negotiate the Bell-Baker trail in my company. Arriving at the Baker house, she shook her head in disgust and set herself and me to work at once cleaning up the mess. The worst of it was flour and sugar spilled from the pots broken in the pantry. March and April rains and humidity had created gluey blobs difficult to mop up. Once Eugenia had seen the extent of the damage, she called Burr Worman's son-in-law and ordered him to meet her Saturday morning on Hudson Road with his tools and with the groceries she had ordered from Burr on the phone. I heard him protesting loudly the condition of the road past the Bell mailbox to her house but she promised to lead him on a short and not too difficult alternative footpath. It took considerable planning to work out the logistics of the next few days. We first had to pack up her clothes and linens in a basket for washing at my home, before leaving her home clean and orderly to return to my home. (I was shocked to realize that I was calling the Bell homestead "home" without a second thought. Wow! What a difference a year on Bald Knob had made in me. Something else I would have to think about when I had time.) The next morning we called the Medical Supply House to come pick up the hospital bed and wheelchair. And the day after that Eugenia, who had graduated to an upstairs bedroom, took a last, long soak in her cherished tub before she and I transported Cassandra home in her cage down the secret trail.

On Saturday I drove us to the Bell mailbox where we found Neil Stevens and his pickup waiting. Eugenia led me (loaded with groceries) and Neil on the promised path to the Bell clearing very easily, very quickly. After Neil had nailed up the sheathing again, fixed broken shelves in the pantry, and installed a hasp and padlock on the door, we all returned to our vehicles on Hudson Road, Neil the richer by $25 dollars for his morning's work. Eugenia and I returned to Bald Knob where we packed up her things and the freshly washed linen we had readied for a return on Sunday morning. As we arrived at the Baker house, Cassie greeted us from the front porch with a smug look on her face and a virulent hiss for Hobo on her lips. I was dumbfounded, "How did she get in? I saw you lock the door."

"Probably through the hole in the roof. That business about her being an indoor cat won't hold water. She's like me, does her own thing in her own way. She might not be able to hunt enough food for herself but I'll keep some dry food on hand. I'm going to start calling Burr to deliver groceries to your mailbox. I'll pick them up there and bring them home. I guess I've had to learn to change my ways and get help when I need it. The biggest problem I'll have is how to pay back all the kindness you and Rosy have lavished on me."

I assured she didn't owe me anything but if she insisted, she could make me a pot to match the one on the hearth in the living room. I went home to tell Rosy that I had Eugenia settled in and she was adapting to her future. Rosy rejoiced for Eugenia and so did I until Rosy dropped the other shoe.

"The agency called and they have a job waiting for me in two weeks, if I want it. I don't know what to tell them. Probably it would be best to take it. With Genie gone, the cleaning service once a month will be adequate and that will save you my salary."

She dredged a Kleenex out of her pocket, wiped her eyes, and blew her nose. "I told them I'd let them know within three days. But I have to tell you I've loved living here with you and Genie and Hobo and Sheba, even Cassie, and having Andy for a friend. It's been just like having a family, but with luxurious living quarters, a spa bathtub, and satellite TV."

I wanted to cry! My face must have reflected my dismay. I, the loner, was suddenly forced to recognize that my happiness and content on Bald Knob was not due to a ritzy salary, comfortable accommodations, interesting walks in the wildwoods, and a wonderful neighbor like Andy. No, I owed happiness to the company of intimate friends and my company might be shrinking. I could be *alone* in the house with only Hobo and Sheba to offset the lonely times.

I gathered my wits, swallowed hard, and spoke through a throat tight with misery, "You'll have to do what you decide is best for you, although I would miss you terribly. You must often have been very bored, marooned up here on Bald Knob, what with Hudson Road restricting your travel. As for you wasting the trust's money, be assured that it and I have got more from you than money's worth. You've given me time to pursue my interests, delicious meals, and what's more, the pleasure of your company. If Hobo and Sheba were able to talk, they would agree."

Turning abruptly, Rosy rushed from the room leaving me *alone* with my unhappiness. Hobo sensed it and whining softly, came to lay his head in my lap. "You're a wonderful companion," I whispered, "but that song Streisand sings about people needing people is very, very true. Let's go for a walk, maybe that will help me weather this disappointment."

Fresh air seemed to clear my brain for useful thinking. I had already made up my mind to urge Eugenia to spend the winter with me at Bald Knob. I had been mentally preparing arguments to spring on her, although I wasn't sure whether she would buy them. If I brought up her age and recent injury, she was sure to counter that she was only a year older than last year when she had spent winter in her own home and she was as spry as ever. If I alluded to the difficulty of her getting supplies, she would say that she had that covered with phone orders to Worman's store. If I told her how I worried about her not being warm enough in her poorly insulated house, she would tell me this winter would be no worse than the 80 some she had already lived through. I plotted a strategy. If I convinced Rosy to stay on, Eugenia might be easier to convince, and if I got Eugenia convinced, Rosy could be convinced that I needed her for the housework. I intended to work on both of them by reminding them I was staying home this winter and I would be lonesome. It wouldn't hurt to try a triple play.

I got back from my walk ready to work first on Rosy. She agreed that having Eugenia live in would free me from housework and give me time for my translation project and studies of Cousin Willy's journals. But it wasn't winter yet and Eugenia hadn't accepted my invitation. I got her to agree to stay on until September. In the end Eugenia said she would think about it and maybe give me an answer in September. Half the battle won, I resigned myself to waiting until September and a second round to win over Eugenia. In the meantime I undertook to teach Rosy the secret Bell-Baker trail and to encourage her to visit Eugenia. I knew they were fond of one another and perhaps by September, living under the same roof would look good to both of them.

I focused especially on Cousin Willy's journals. A survey of the desk drawer counted up four rows of books, packed six books to a row, and a fifth partial row. The books in the partial row were the most recent. I read backwards, numbering each as I finished. Still very few or no dates but Willy often referred to the season in which he was writing and I guesstimated that a full row might account for 15 to 18 years of entries. Poring over Willy's minuscule printing was hard labor. I purchased a special mounted magnifier at the stationery store in Greenwood and that was some help. In May I had covered the journal contents to a time when Andy's name no longer appeared. I found the first time Willy and Andy had met in Amsterdam and pinned that down with Andy's memory to July of 1998. My respect for the man William Bell grew with every page. He was witty, well-read, insightful and delightfully opinionated. Reading Thomas Friedman's *The World is Flat* he commented, "He is so right except that I liked it better when it was round. When I was a boy it took longer for bad news to circulate and the good news was better when it came."

I plugged patiently along, interrupting the chore only for eating, sleeping, walking with Hobo, and dinners with Andy, Rosy, and Eugenia. Then one day in July, I came across these words: "Amanda died today. She was a good woman and loving sister." I was able to date that entry to November, 1989, from her gravestone. Eugenia told me about Amanda with a tear in her eye. "She was an old maid, kept Willy's house faithfully while he gallivanted all over the world, fed and put up with his guests, and bolstered his ego whenever he had a fit of what he called the blue devils. She and I were good friends." She had apparently been in poor health for several months before she died, but Willy noted "she never complained."

In August, I found an entry dated Essen, Spring, that cited Herr Kammer's happiness with the installation of the new devices in his smokestacks, says he intends to ask the German Engineering Society for a commendation. Two lines followed: "Amanda wired me that Lou packed up and left. Foolish, foolish, only six months along." I reread lines ahead and after but found no additional comment. So I took my question to Eugenia as we sat on the bench under her giant maple tree. "If Lou was my mother Louise and she was six months pregnant when she packed up and left Bald Knob, she was carrying me. What's the story? And what has it to do with the scandal you mentioned once?"

Eugenia blinked and paused for a long moment before answering. "Is that all Willy put in his journal? He said he wrote it all down but maybe it's not in the journal. The scandal hit him and Amanda pretty hard. Amanda told me all about it but warned me not to let Willy know she had."

"Well, everybody's dead now, I think I deserve to know. Come on."

"I think too you ought to know. It's not pretty but now that I know you and how well you've turned out, I guess the truth won't cause you or anyone else any damage. It's like this:

"Wilfred Bell and his half-sister Bella were Willy's cousins. I knew both of them because me and my brothers and sisters played with them when they came to spend summers at Bald Knob. Wilfred and Bella were both brilliant, Wilfred went on to make millions in business and Bella was a poet and a good one. She ran away from home when she was 18, ended up in Philadelphia, had twin children without benefit of marriage, died of something when the kids were four. The kids got sent to Wilfred and his wife, Hattie, in Cincinnati. Living in Wilfred's house was probably comfortable but Hattie wasn't much for nurturing. Louise and Victor were packed off to Bald Knob every year from May to October for Amanda to look after. She loved them with her whole heart. Willy was fond of them and spent a lot of time with them when he was around.

"Wilfred had been in the Army Reserve. After a tour of duty to Viet Nam he came back a hero with medals and commendations, but he was a changed man, given to cruel rages and ranting. Sometimes he was so upset he didn't remember afterwards what he had done or said. His behavior was another reason the kids were sent off to Bald Knob. Meanwhile the kids grew up. Victor went to college in Columbus, Louise to some local college in Cincinnati. The scandal was that Wilfred in one of his crazy spells raped Louise, and when Victor found out about it and confronted Wilfred, there was gunplay.

Wilfred shot Victor and then shot himself. Hattie couldn't get rid of Louise fast enough when she found out about the pregnancy, sent her to Bald Knob."

I sat there with my mouth hanging open, unable to believe my ears. When I could get the words out, I said, "Are you telling me that my father raped his niece, my mother, killed my uncle and himself? That I was born because of rape, incest, and murder?"

"Louise was only his half-niece." Eugenia said mildly, "Amanda said it was like a Greek tragedy worthy of some play writer named Ess-ke-lus. I didn't know who she was talking about, but I had to agree it was tragedy! I hope all this doesn't upset you. It was so many years ago and everybody is dead now."

"Aeschylus or O'Neill. No, I'm not upset. Surprised, but I've always known the father line on my birth certificate was blank. It never bothered me or held me back that I had no father but of course, I've always wondered. Just think, the tragedy wasn't over until my mother Louise died in that horrible industrial fire, and others with her. Why didn't Willy know about me for years after she died?"

"He probably knew but if he didn't know until after Amanda died, he likely left well enough alone. You were in a loving foster home and bringing you to Bald Knob with no woman to look after you wouldn't have been a good solution. It wasn't until he expected to die that he got the idea in his head to find you and give you the job of looking after the Bell homestead and Hobo. He told me he had engaged a private detective to find you and his lawyers to make that peculiar arrangement. Willy wasn't an ordinary man and he didn't think in ordinary ways. So here you are."

"Yes, I've been very lucky, haven't I? Shielded from knowledge of all the tragedies, kindly reared by good folk, and educated until I was grown and able to look after myself. I can't complain or blame anyone, even Willy. So far his crazy idea has given me a lot of happiness and content."

I reached over and hugged Eugenia, held her tight, and kissed her on the cheek. Hobo got up and came to lean against my knee. He wasn't accustomed to such displays of affection. He understood handshakes but not hugs and kisses.

I went home from Eugenia's house musing with every step on the astonishing story I had heard. I wasn't playing nice-nice when I assured Eugenia I wasn't upset. I truly wasn't. Surprised, maybe a little shocked, certainly touched, but not upset. I felt sorry for my mother, struggling to keep me in home and health, victim twice over, of heinous crime and dreadful circumstance. I think I loved the memory of her more now than I did before I knew of her troubles. Knowing myself as a child of tragedy—father, uncle, mother, even the Conrads—had I survived a Homeric curse? Were the lords of Olympus finally satisfied? It really made no difference, I knew who I was and that was enough.

I wondered if I still might find Willy's version of the story among papers he had stashed away. Maybe I was more regretful than ever that Willy was dead and I couldn't ask him why he didn't approach me while he was alive. Whatever, I was not going to brood on my new knowledge nor did I intend to spread it around. All those dead people deserved a respectful privacy. I was even lighthearted enough to sing a wordless tune as I threw sticks for Hobo to retrieve.

I went back to Cousin Willy's journals with new interest, hoping to find perhaps a few words about Louise in happier days. Besides, the mystery of my birth having been solved there yet remained another, the combination of that monumental safe. I had inquired of O'Leary whether it was among the legal papers of the estate but he had just chuckled and said he would have to hire a safecracker if the need arose to see the contents of the safe. I had little or no hope of finding an explicit or a coded reference to that combination in the journals but Cousin Willy was just devious enough to provide a surprise somewhere sometime.

August came with searing heat and drought. On Bald Knob the daytime winds scorched my skin and Hobo's lungs. We stayed in the air conditioning most of the time. Local news emphasized the risk of forest fires and the sheriff sent deputies to alert every house in wooded areas of the county. If Hobo and I walked at all, we did so in the early morning or late evening. Daily I scanned the skies over the forests around Bald Knob with binoculars watching for smoke. Finally relief of the heat arrived. Three consecutive days of crashing thunderstorms and howling winds took down every vulnerable tree, but left sparkling, clear blue skies and cool, refreshing air behind. Hobo and I celebrated the first day of good weather with a ramble to inspect most of our favorite trails. Although none was blocked, twigs and small branches occasionally choked narrow areas.

The evening of August 18 was so delightful that I opened the windows of the front-corner bedroom (I was still uncomfortable calling it my room) when I went to bed around 10. I woke around midnight to the sound of a vehicle on Hudson Road. Occasionally, someone took a right turn in Corona, mistaking Hudson Road for another crossroad farther to the north. The Bell mailbox was the first place wide enough for a turnaround, and the cliffs always muted the sound of their departure. So I turned over ready for sleep again. But a while later I heard the scrabble of Hobo's feet on the stairs and in the downstairs hall.

A sudden outburst of barks coupled with a scuffle and smothered cries featuring male voices warned me of one or more intruders. I was shocked. I always faithfully followed Andy's advice to lock doors. Strangers in the house had to be breaking in. Quickly I rose and slipped on a pair of moccasins, donned a flannel robe, and crept soundlessly down the stairs. At the foot I was reaching for the light switch when I heard a shot and saw the beam of a flashlight swinging across the door to Cousin Willy's workrooms. I also saw Hobo lying motionless on the floor. Although I was almost paralyzed with horror and fear, I kept my presence of mind. In the dark, I moved into the office, and fumbled silently to take out the Glock from the desk drawer. I had practiced shooting that day and contrary to Andy's advice and my usual habit, had put up the gun loaded and not cleaned. I intended to practice again tomorrow but now I was ready to deal with burglars. Just then, Rosy, at the foot of the stairs, was calling my name and turning on the light.

"Becca? I heard a shot. You're not in your room. What's going on? Oh, my God! Hobo!"

I scurried out of the office and down the hall, past Hobo's lifeless body. By now the burglars had broken through the lock on the inside door and turned on the lights in the file room. Two men, in black from head to toe, were standing in front of the safe with a tool box on the floor between them. There was no doubt in my mind as to their intentions. I fired once and one of the men yelped, flesh wound maybe. My hand was shaking, but I fired a second time and saw chips of plaster fly off the wall. The other man turned toward me, I thought I saw a gun in his hand, I stopped shaking, and the third time I shot to do deadly harm. He howled in pain and he and his pal ran for the door, bowling me over as they left through the front door. I could hear their feet scrambling over the gravel of the parking lot and see the beam of a flashlight dancing in the direction of the drive.

I turned around to see Rosy at the kitchen phone. "I've called 9-1-1," she said. "Are they gone?"

I was on my knees by Hobo, my ear pressed to his chest. His heart was still beating but blood was dripping from his head. He must still be alive. "Rosy, get my purse. It's on the desk in the office. I've got to get Hobo to a vet as fast as I can."

"But you're not dressed!"

I wasn't listening. I was gathering Hobo up in my arms and in spite of his 70 odd pounds was carrying him across the parking lot to the barn and the Cherokee. By the time I had put him on the back seat and backed the car out, Rosy was standing with my purse in one hand and the Glock in the other.

"What shall I do with the gun? Oh my God, what if they come back? Oh, oh, oh."

"Give me that purse and if they come back, shoot 'em."

I was in the driver's seat and down the lane to Hudson Road as fast as I could go, then around the twists and turns of Hudson Road and on the road to Greenwood. I stopped for a minute in Corona and dialed Dr. Mac's emergency number. His answering service responded immediately and she said she would relay my message. At the outskirts of Greenwood, I saw Hobo in the rear view mirror struggling to rise and falling back. I poured it on through the sleeping streets of the town to find Dr. Mac at the clinic door, all the lights on, in scrubs and ready for us. He lifted Hobo out and within minutes had him stretched on a treatment table. I had to sit down; I was drained of energy but frantic with worry. I watched as if in a dream as Dr. Mac's gentle hands moved over Hobo's flaccid body. At last, Dr. Mac looked up with a smile.

"Good news! The bullet was small caliber. After grazing his skull, it went on and entered the muscle of his haunch. I can feel it just under the skin. I'll do x-rays to make sure. He's suffering concussion and should come around fairly soon. Although he's bleeding a bit, all his vital signs are good."

I emptied my lungs of pent up air in one great whoosh and sagged in my chair. With blurred vision I saw Hobo beginning to stir weakly. He was trying to get on his feet but Dr. Mac was preparing a shot of something.

"I'm going to put him into a light sleep while I take out the bullet. Why don't you go out to the waiting room? I'll come to you when it's over."

"Keep the bullet," I remembered to say. "The sheriff's people will want it for evidence."

I sat on a hard bench, slumping against the wall, and fell asleep. It was 4 A.M. when Dr. Mac woke me. He told me I could go home and come back tomorrow when Hobo was likely able to go home. I asked to see Hobo and dropped a lot of tears on the bandages over his unconscious body. When I called home to report on Hobo's condition, Rosy told me to hurry on home, she would have the coffee pot going and breakfast ready for Andy and me. Andy greeted me with a hug and silent sympathy.

"Rosy called to tell me what had happened. I was shocked," he said, "but I have to compliment you on your presence of mind. Your shooting lessons have paid off. I expected locked doors to give you adequate security and on Hankin backing off after O'Leary read him the riot act. Now, there's no telling who is behind this latest attempt but to me it looks like a professional job. The front door lock had been picked and the workroom door lock had been blown out with some kind of plastic explosive."

Rosy chimed in, "I called the sheriff and he sent deputies to search Hudson Road and the lot for tire tracks. They're coming back at daylight for fingerprints. We're not supposed to touch anything in the meantime."

I managed to choke down some toast and a cup of coffee. Two aspirins didn't calm me down so I stripped off my bloodied robe, and decided to lie down and perhaps sleep. Hobo was going to be all right but at what a cost! I prayed that the shots I got off at the burglars were causing them great pain and blood loss. I knew I had hit both of them. I almost wished they had shot me and not my dog. There, I admit Hobo had me by the heart strings. Cousin Willy probably counted on that when he planned his scheme.

I woke to find Rosy jogging my shoulder and apologizing for waking me.

"That nice Deputy Roth wants to ask you some questions. Dr. Mac called and Hobo is doing great."

"What time is it?" I asked groggily.

"Noon. I made some hearty chicken broth for you when you're ready for it. It will settle your stomach. Do you want it before or after you talk to the deputy?"

I crawled out of bed, showered quickly, and dressed. In spite of feeling like I was walking on rubber balls as I went down the stairs, I managed not to stumble. Deputy Roth was sitting at the kitchen table, cup of tea and notebook in hand. The questions she asked were to be expected. My answers were not particularly helpful, the only description I could give of the burglars amounted to one tall and skinny, the other short and stocky, both in black pants, turtleneck tops, ski masks. I summed up my actions: I got off three shots after the lights were on, first hitting the leg of the short one, then a spot on the wall, next hitting somewhere on the body of the tall one. The deputy had already recreated the shootings from the shell casings, the blood trails, and Rosy's tale of the event. What I thought was a gun in the hand of the tall guy must have been a portable drill. It was found on the floor in a puddle of blood and next to the outline of a box of some sort.

"A tool box," I said, "I saw it clearly. It was dark green."

The deputy said it probably departed with the burglars. "The blood gave us shoeprints and the drill was good for the fingerprints of at least one of the men, most likely the tall one. Do you know who shot your dog?"

"When Hobo was shot, the only light in the hall was the beam from their flashlight. So I didn't see the shooter, but Dr. Mac saved the bullet."

My head was swimming—I was woozy not only because I was short of food and sleep, but because I now fully realized that I had inflicted bodily harm on human targets instead of an old oak tree. With my elbows on the table I dropped my head into my hands to steady myself. Rosy took command, setting a bowl of warm broth and a spoon under my nose, and insisting I eat. The deputy took pity on me and said she probably had as much information as I could provide for the moment. She told us her partner had the burglar's shell casing and was stopping at the vet clinic to pick up the bullet. Reminding me that I had no license for the Glock, she was taking it with her as evidence. When she left, I was too busy scooping up soup to bid her good-bye. It took another two hours and a ham sandwich before I had recovered enough to go after Hobo. Andy had volunteered but I felt I should be responsible.

When the vet tech led Hobo from the kennel area, he was limping and disfigured by patches of shaven skin on his head, flank, and hip. One or two stitches crossed the graze on his head and several more stitches closed the bullet's track on his flank. But his tail waved vigorous greeting, he interrupted his limp with a clumsy cavort, and he hustled to lay his head in my lap. I slid off the chair to the floor and wrapped my arms around him in a careful embrace that earned a lavish face wash. Dr. Mac was laughing when he came from the back room. "Happy reunion, I'd say. Lucky you, lucky dog. The deputy came by and I turned over the bullet to him."

I was caressing Hobo with a deep massage of his neck to avoid his wounds. "There's something lumpy here. I know he has a chip but there's something else. Are you sure there was only one bullet?"

"Hey, I do good work. I didn't miss a thing. Hobo has always had two chips. His chart says one of them registers him to the national database, and the other was put in at the request of his owner."

"What did Mr. Willy have in mind? Can you read both of them?"

"Yes, the registration chip is 9 numbers in 3 sets, three digits each, separated by dots. The other is a mixture of digits and letters. You may want to write it down. My note says it was provided by Mr. Bell. It reads R10B35R65B3."

"What do you suppose that means?"

"Haven't the faintest idea. I didn't ask and Mr. Bell didn't volunteer."

More of Cousin Willy's tricks, I thought. I wrote the readings on a scrap of paper and put the paper in my purse. The odd reading must have meaning but I'll have to search further among his papers to find out what. My weary brain refused to think more about it at the moment. Now I just wanted to get Hobo home.

With the paper work done, the vet tech led Hobo to the car, lifted him into the passenger seat, and handed me a plastic bag of antibiotic ointment and instructions for dressing the wounds. We headed for home. As we went my dog was assessing the scenery, I was happily humming along to the golden oldies playing on the radio. Andy was waiting to lift Hobo out of the car although Hobo would have been happy to jump down by himself. Once on the ground he made a round of all his watering places and refreshed their scents. Panting joyously, he hobbled up the veranda steps ahead of us to greet Rosy. When we entered we found Eugenia putting the finishing touches on a gala dinner.

"Where's Sheba?" I asked. "Seems like I haven't seen her in days."

Rosy laughed and informed me that Sheba was spending all her time, aside from necessary food and elimination sessions, hiding under my bed on Hobo's rug. I led him to the foot of the stairs and commanded him to speak. A single ARF brought Sheba flying out from under the bed and down the stairs to give him a frenzied greeting, licking his face and sniffing his stitches, purring and meowing madly. She must have been frightened by the shooting and worried by Hobo's absence, but his return put all right with her world. After he laid down at the kitchen door, Sheba cuddled between his front legs, still purring like a train.

Andy had just finished a temporary repair on the front door. Until a locksmith could come and change the locks front and back, a sturdy bar slotted through brackets bolted into the door jambs was to be our security. Andy said I would have to decide what to do about the lock on the file room door. He gave me the name and phone number of a licensed locksmith and insisted that I call him tomorrow. I had no idea what I should do about overall security and suddenly remembered I hadn't reported to B.O.&S about the break-in. I'd do that tomorrow also because a glance at the clock told me the robot was in command of the phone line.

Eugenia and Rosy had prepared an extravaganza of meatloaf, mashed potatoes and gravy, peas and carrots, to which we all sat down and for which we said heartfelt grace. Rosy had brought Eugenia up to date on the "doings" of the past 24 hours and she had come prepared to spend the night. We finished up the day in the big living room with coffee and SaraLee cheesecake. Andy took his leave but before departing he fussed over the door, showed me how to adjust it, hugged me in a reassuring fashion, and planted a comradely kiss on my forehead. I felt an uncomfortable sense of loss as I watched the beams of his ATV headlights fade into the darkness.

O'Leary listened to my tale of events without comment but he had advice and an announcement before we signed off.

"Get your house door locks in order but don't bother about the workroom door yet. I think it's time Bender and I paid a site visit to Bald Knob. Ben has never been there and it's been three years since I was. We can have a general pow-wow and make some decisions for future security. If all those bedrooms are still available, Ben and I will plan an overnight stay. OK?"

"Certainly, we'll love to have you! Just say when.'"

"I have some commitments on my calendar but it looks like next Wednesday is free. How's that? We'll get there around noon and leave the following morning. How's Hobo doing?"

"Healing, happy to be home. The vet promised his limp will pass in a week or so. Thanks for asking."

With the schedule set, I asked Andy to be available for the afternoon and evening next Wednesday. Rosy and I turned out the linen closets of the unused bedrooms, washed up the linens, and made up the beds. I had to laugh; Cousin Willy's crazy notion to provide himself with plenty of guest rooms was paying off. I planned to invite Eugenia to join us and stay over so she could meet my backup team. There was still a room available for a drop-in, or for Andy if he wanted to stay. We laid in ample provisions from the Greenwood A&P and planned a nice menu for dinner guests. It was fun! I had never lived in circumstances with resources for overnight guests, not even when I lived with the Conrads. I foresaw a novel and welcome experience.

Bender and O'Leary arrived about 11 A.M. driving a black Buick four-door sedan. They were dressed for a weekend in the woods, heavy shoes, red plaid flannel shirts, and matching red plaid caps. They toted canvas ditty bags. I was amused. We were not so far off the beaten path as to justify Bunyanesque garb but I thought, what the hey, whatever turned them on. Hobo, Rosy, and I met them at the door. After the introductions with handshakes, full names, and honorifics, I decided informality would make the visit much easier.

"Now, I want to say, I'm not Miss Bell and this is not Mrs. Rosenbaum, we are Becca and Rosy."

O'Leary was rather taken aback but he rallied, "OK, then we are Dan and Ben."

"Come in and I'll show you to your rooms." I led them to the stairs and down the upstairs hall. "I've made Cousin Willy's room mine, and Rosy's is next to it, then there's the one we keep for Eugenia. You will recall Mrs. Baker was a houseguest this past winter. She often comes for dinner by daylight over a demanding trail, and since I won't let her return on that trail in the dark, she stays the night. You gentlemen may take your picks from the three remaining rooms."

Dan laughed, "I recall I asked Mr. Bell about all these bedrooms. He chuckled and shrugged and said 'You can never tell when you'll need one.' Do you suppose he foresaw the extent of your hospitality?"

"I'm mighty glad if he did. I always thought of myself as a loner but I've certainly been grateful for the friends I've made here on Bald Knob. Take your time to freshen up. We'll have lunch when you come down."

Not unexpectedly lunch conversation revolved around the state of Hudson Road. Ben had been the driver and he confessed to his heart in his mouth the whole way on the ascent. "Cliffs on one side, sheer dropoffs on the other, heavy foliage looming over blind curves, potholes, crumbling berms—I can't imagine you racing in the dark to get Hobo to the vet. That road is a major challenge in the daytime, it had to be more so at night. Can't the county do something about it?"

I laughed. "They have. Didn't you notice the barricade and warning sign just past the Bell mailbox?"

"Barricade and sign ROAD CLOSED IMPASSABLE should be posted as the road leaves Corona." Rosy chimed in. "I drove my car up here to take up this job and now I'm here, I doubt I'll drive it down. I've never gone down since except as a passenger with my eyes closed and jaws locked."

I felt obliged to defend or at least explain the problem. "It's not so bad when you are used to it. I drive it down and up at least once a week. At the moment the pavement is in pretty good shape. Early spring and winter are the worst times. When I checked on it with the county surveyor, I was told Hudson Road was on the list for improvement but low priority because it serves only Bald Knob and the Baker homestead. The cost, you see. And most of the time the road keeps out undesirables. Of course, not always, since burglars and Hankins's minions seem to take it in stride."

Lunch over, Dan asked for a re-enactment of the mayhem of our recent horrific event. My emotions were as uneasy when I led the parade as they had been when I had done so for the deputies. Rosy's and Hobo's memories were as uncomfortable as mine but like good sports, both replayed their roles faithfully. Opening the shattered door of Cousin Willy's file room, I noticed that Ben's golf tan turned a bit greenish at the sight of the bloody mess inside. Dan took it in stride. Rosy and Hobo had withdrawn discreetly to the kitchen.

I felt obliged to apologize, "The deputies let Rosy and me clean up the hall but not this room; it's still a crime scene. So just look and don't touch anything, please."

Thankfully, the look was brief and Dan, Ben, Hobo, and I were soon seated in front of the living room fireplace, all of us silent and lost in thought. Dan finally drew a long breath and broke the silence.

"Your presence of mind in dealing with the burglars was unbelievable, and your target practice definitely paid off. What was a painful experience and has undoubtedly turned into an even more painful memory. It boggles my mind that William Bell, never having met you, could be so certain that as a Bell you could cope with whatever difficulty life handed you. I salute you and him as well."

I could feel myself blushing, but since I had no reply, I just leaned down and rubbed Hobo's neck. I was about to mention to Dan the discovery of Hobo's extra chip, but I was distracted when Dan asked Ben to give him and me time alone. "Maybe," he said, "you can take a walk in this fine weather or look over the library while Becca and I talk privately." What in the world, I wondered, needed to be discussed privately. As far as I knew, Ben knew everything about my special status as tenant of the Bell homestead and caretaker of Hobo and the contract that I had signed. Ben didn't seem put out by Dan's suggestion but to ease the situation, I suggested Dan and I could settle down in Cousin Willy's office for our talk.

Without thinking, I sat down behind the desk and waved Dan to a chair on the other side. I hit the switch for the overhead light that illuminated the desktop. I was a bit shocked when I realized I had assumed control of the meeting. But taking Cousin Willy's chair had become natural.

"You've already praised me. Now are you about to scold?"

Laughing, Dan replied. "No, I want first to ask you some questions. Three up front that you can probably answer in one paragraph: Is your salary adequate? Is the house satisfactory? I'm pretty sure of the answer to the next one. Are you and Hobo good friends?"

"Last asked, first answered, Hobo and I are *best* friends! As to salary, I have more money than I know what to do with. I'm contemplating checking with a financial consultant about investing most of my humongous bank account. As for the house, weird as it is, now that I've rearranged the furniture and purchased a few pieces with my own money, I'm perfectly happy. But I confess to looking forward to having the security system back in order."

"You had a house guest this past winter. How did that work out?"

"No expense! Eugenia's hospitalization, nurse, rental of hospital bed and wheel chair were all covered by her Medicare. My expenses are groceries, gas for the car, and a few clothes. I don't have Hobo's vet bill yet but Dr. Mac said it won't be much more than $500. Ben pays Rosy's salary and I expect will pay for the locksmith and whatever security services we decide on."

"You've dealt with quite a round of problems in the 28 months you've lived here: the prowlers of The Patriot Guard, Hankins's people probing for weaknesses, the break-in and vandalizing of Mrs. Baker's house, and now this outright attack. How are you feeling about them?" Dan's expression made me think he was bracing for the worst.

"The Patriot Guard is no longer a problem and is not likely to return. The General or Colonel, whatever he calls himself, found a place for his training site elsewhere, in another county 50 miles away. He was motivated partly by law enforcement's close surveillance in this county and partly by bad publicity created by the arrests of the Guards responsible for breaking into Eugenia's house. Fingerprints in her house identified one of the guys on a fugitive warrant from Marion County and he's in jail over there on a major felony rap. He ratted on the other one who is in jail in this county awaiting trial on the Baker thing and some additional counts. I'm convinced that The Patriot Guard in this area is a spent force."

"That seems to eliminate them from this recent event at Bald Knob. I can tell you that I am pretty sure Hankins is not involved. My talk with him left him thinking hard about the FBI and other agencies of Homeland Security. Besides, although he's a sneaky son of a B..., anything he tries is likely to avoid overt violence. I think he too is a spent force. That leaves the current problem."

I shifted uneasily in my chair. "Yes, the worst one. However, I met yesterday with the sheriff and the deputies on the case. I had never told them of Hankins's efforts until now but they immediately dismissed industrial espionage as a cause. Their current task force has been working on house invasions, half a dozen in the past few months. The invasions focus on "soft" targets, wealthy residences temporarily unoccupied or occupied by vulnerable owners, and known to have safes for valuables. The detectives have spotted a link common to all of them, *including this one*, a tradesman named Roland Schell who does electrical wiring to install televisions and home entertainment systems. His brother-in-law, a man named Jonas, was released a year ago from the state prison in Michigan City when he completed a sentence for breaking and entering and safecracking. His crimes have not so far involved gunplay, but Jonas might well have learned its usefulness from his prison mates and have enlisted Schell for this break-in. Schell is a registered gun owner of a Beretta 9 mm and shoots target at shows."

"What is the sheriff waiting for?" Dan's anger burst out. "He has Hobo's bullet, doesn't he? There are surely matching bullets to find in Schell's show targets!"

"They want Jonas, too, so they're waiting for the state and FBI reports of fingerprints on the drill and DNA matches of the blood from the guys I shot. They are quite confident all their evidence will add up to a solid case. They just want to be sure before they act. They have also found a male admission to a Kentucky hospital for a gunshot wound to the chest and overnight stay for treatment, but the name is probably faked and they don't have the bullet yet. They want to try a match to my gun but the bullet is tied up in red tape negotiations with Kentucky cops. Everything is in progress. The probability of apprehension of the culprits and felony charges is high. I left the meeting sworn to secrecy and cautioned to be patient."

"Well, your news is encouraging. So much so that I am encouraged to bring up an important topic that both affects and doesn't affect you. What do you say to a cup of coffee or a soda before I start?"

I said yes and went off to the kitchen for the drinks.

Dan took a big swig of his soda and cleared his throat before beginning.

"I asked Ben to be elsewhere because I am not yet free to let him in on some negotiations that have begun between an important American company and the Bell Trust. A few years ago William Bell approached American Innovation Metals, or more conveniently A-I-M *AIM,* with a revolutionary metals-processing device. At the time, the company's operations were very conservative and not particularly profitable. Certain members of the board were trying to get new blood and new thinking into operations. They believed the company should take some risk and live up to the innovation its name implied. But they were up against a stick-in-the-mud CEO and recalcitrant CFO, neither of whom they had the guts to fire. When times got bad and profits fell nearly to zero, the board grabbed the opportunity to take major steps to restructure the company. A go-get-'em CEO has the company on a new and promising path; it now wants the technology it turned down three years ago and is willing to pay for it. AIM has approached the Bell estate, now the Bell trust, with offers to acquire the entire body of William Bell's technical work, including its current licenses. The trust is seriously considering the offers. The terms and amounts under discussion could significantly increase the holdings as well as the long-term income of the trust."

I was growing somewhat impatient with Dan's deliberate oratory. Get to the point, I was thinking. I almost asked what has this corporate horsing around got to do with me but I refrained.

Dan continued. "The reason that the sale of William Bell's technical property has *nothing* to do with you is that your contract is with the trust and will continue to be valid regardless of the trust's decision. At the same time, for two reasons a sale *could have* a great deal to do with you. One, removal of the technical property currently located in this house would relieve you of the responsibility of caretaker. Your peace of mind would be immeasurably increased."

"Sounds good to me," I blurted out. "Living here without the dread of attack would be great! I know I have no voice in the trust's decision but if I did, I'd be picketing it with SELL signs. The stuff is no good to me and the responsibility has been nothing but trouble."

"There's also the second reason and it's a big one! Remember that according to the terms of your contract, the trust becomes your unrestricted inheritance upon Hobo's natural death. An out-and-out sale of the Bell package will increase the total worth of the trust and consequently the amount of your potential inheritance. However, if negotiations should lead to the trust becoming a part owner of AIM and recipient of income from profits accruing from that arrangement—AIM's success stands to benefit your inheritance or conversely, AIM's failure would risk a part of it."

"Dan, I couldn't care less about a lot of money. In the abstract, stony broke and filthy rich are about the same to me. I admit that I don't want to end up homeless and hungry but as long as I can earn my way, I never will. It's nice to live as comfortably as I now am in this nice house and with a big salary. But it's not a be-all and end-all for me."

An involuntary sob choked me as I continued. "If Hobo dies or is killed, that would break my heart. If lose the friendship of Eugenia or Roxy or Andy, I'd be bereft, but I'd survive. I know now I can form new friendships and live a meaningful life. So why are you bothering me with the maybes and what-ifs? You'd better be worrying about how you're going to get Cousin Willy's safe open if the negotiations with AIM go to the wire. If they buy all or part of Willy's stuff, they'll certainly want what's in that safe and as far as I know, no one knows how to get it without blasting and that could wreck what's inside!"

"OK, I grant that getting that safe open will be crucial but at the moment I have only two considerations: one, working out a viable deal with AIM; and two, making sure you understand what's at stake for you personally. I believe your declaration of independence from financial considerations. I'll see to getting the safe open when push comes to shove in our negotiations with AIM. In the meantime, please continue delving through William Bell's desiderata for clues."

He laughed, "I've always wanted to use that word, *desiderata*, in a sentence. I hope I used it properly."

I joined in his laughter. Our serious conversation seemed to be over. I gave him a glimpse of the full drawer of journals and pointed out those still unread. I showed him the contents of file folders that I had already sifted without finding anything substantial. We both sighed and decided the good smells coming from the kitchen were signs of dinner.

Eugenia had arrived while Dan and I conferred. When we left the office, we found her entertaining Ben with stories of Bald Knob and the Baker lands in her childhood. Dan and I heard only the end of the story of fire that had taken out the grist mill but we got the full treatment of the man who brought his three muscular sons and a yoke of oxen to carry away the millstones on his dray. "Now that was recycling!" she emphasized.

Dan, Ben, and I sat watching while Rosy and Eugenia put the finishing touches on the menu. Rosy hovered over a huge roast of beef resting prior to carving and Eugenia mashed potatoes with panache and a running commentary. When Andy came he took charge of the wine and brought up prize-winning French Merlot and a white dessert wine that smelled like flowers when he opened it. I was never sure whether all the formal introductions had been made, but whether or not, conversation flourished.

It was a convivial group that surrounded the table in the kitchen. Rosy had resurrected a fine linen tablecloth and matching napkins from some linen closet and she and Eugenia had set it with the colorful dishware from the hutch. A further rummage in the kitchen cupboards had found wineglasses and a set of chunky candleholders to further bedeck the table. Once the cutlery was added to the six settings, there was scarcely space for serving dishes. But we all sat down and exhibited our trencher talents. Conversation continued.

I became particularly impressed with Andy's company manners. He talked knowledgeably with Ben about currently hot commodities and with Dan about a recent controversial ruling by the Indiana Supreme Court. Ben was sure gas would find a more stable and lower price very soon and Eugenia (who now possessed a radio and listened to it) expressed her firm opinion that it better come down before it pushed the country into a new depression. When politics took center stage, Rosy had a funny story. Her husband, Izzy the tailor, had made a fine new suit for a guy who had decided to run for a Congressional seat. The first time the guy wore his suit to a political rally, he speechified so energetically, waving his arms in vigorous oratory, that he split out the armhole seams. When he brought the suit back to Izzy for repair, Izzy suggested running on the Democratic ticket, because Democrats are already convinced that privatizing Medicare is a loony idea. When the guy caught on to Izzy's political leanings, he refused to pay him for the repairs.

Dan already knew and approved of Andy; he now was quite taken with Eugenia and Rosy. He later told me privately I had lucked out with lively and interesting friends. He understood why I was happy in the boondocks; the company was so good that I didn't need city folks for stimulation. Dan and I had one more conference the following morning. Mostly he was reassuring himself that I was happy with the status quo and didn't give a hoot about an inheritance that might rival a Buffett or Gates portfolio. I promised to keep searching for the combination of Cousin Willy's safe. I told Dan that Willy had once joked with Andy that only Hobo knew the combination. Hobo was sitting at my side and pricked his ears at the mention of his name, but volunteered not even an ARF. As Dan and I talked, I took a call from Deputy Roth lifting the designation of crime scene from Cousin Willy's workrooms. "Scrub away all you like," she said cheerfully, "better you than me!"

Ben and Dan left after lunching on cold roast beef sandwiches and carrying a paper bag of them for snacking as they traveled to Columbia. Eugenia had gone home early in the day. All the guests gone, Rosy and I mustered buckets and mops, rags and brushes, and tackled the mess in the outer workroom, mopping and scrubbing blood splashed on the floors and splattered liberally on the file cabinets. We put up our cleaning equipment at 5 P.M. and congratulated ourselves on the spiffy job we had done. The next day I had a call from the Diebolt man who was coming next Monday to install a new lock on the outer wooden door and a new steel inner door and lock. He would also examine the safe and recommend to Dan a strategy for opening it.

I went back to Cousin Willy's files in the hope that somewhere he had recorded a combination for the safe. I did find a copy of a letter he had written to the Diebolt company some years ago, in which he announced a technique to reset the combination of a safe's lock, useful in case of a lost or forgotten combination and thereby avoiding drastic means of entry. "I am prepared to sell this technique to the Diebolt company for $100,000. Contact me if you are interested." An answer from a company official contained a rather starchy refusal. "We do not believe it to our advantage to consider such means. As a matter of policy, we consider resetting a combination ill-advised and likely to be abused by users of our safety devices." Scribbled across the bottom of this letter was a comment, "Arrogant bastard!"

I spent sometime on the contents of a file labeled "Hobo." It consisted of a correspondence with a Mrs. Grace Moore of the Glen Moore Kennels, breeder of pedigreed Alsatians, located in Macon, Georgia. Willy's letter announced Hobo's death at the age of twelve and his intention to obtain a puppy to take his place. Her reply informed him. "We have presently three male puppies, bred from the same strain as your last Hobo, and of an age suitable for adoption. These puppies are being socialized and trained in the basics by my daughter. She reports that each of them displays excellent temperament and intelligence. I suggest you visit to look them over and make a choice." Cousin Willy replied to set up a date. A later letter thanked Mrs. Moore for the opportunity to obtain the current Hobo and reported his rapid adjustment to his new master. The folder also contained the AKC registration papers and Hobo's pedigree. It appeared he had been born Prinz Alfred, May 5, 2007, the offspring of Baron Waldemar and Grafin Gertrude von Speyer. Hobo's illustrious origin amused me. He was at the moment slouching beside me, one leg cocked up high to facilitate a vigorous search for a flea that he must have picked up on our last walk. "OK, old boy, I'll give you a good brushing before bedtime," I promised. As I rubbed his neck, I felt again the two chips and wondered why Cousin Willy had so endowed him. I pawed through the loose papers I had allowed to accumulate on the desk, looking for the scrap of paper where I had scribbled the cryptic reading Dr. Mac had found for the extra chip. R10B35R65B3 was an odd combination of letters and numbers. Not for the first time I wondered at its meaning but now I decided Hobo's folder was the place for this scrap of paper.

The man from Diebolt arrived in small blue panel truck at the dot of 12 noon of the appointed day and parked at the foot of the veranda steps. Seeing him get out of the truck, I thought he looked just like one of those gnomes some people plant in their flower beds. He was barely five feet tall, rotund, bald, with a tonsure of frizzy gray hair, bushy eyebrows and a goatee. He stomped up the stairs, ignoring my outstretched hand, and said, "Please show me your driver's license." I stuttered something to the effect that I had to go find my wallet first.

"Sorry," he snapped. "Company policy. We have to be sure that the party responsible for the security device is the party requesting our services." When I handed him my license, he pulled out a pair of granny glasses and peered carefully at the photo.

"Humph, the picture doesn't do you justice, Miss Bell, but I daresay that's to be expected."

He handed my license back and then passed me a set of cards: his driver's license with photo i.d., a company badge with photo i.d., a laminated certificate with photo i.d. and numbers of a bond and license for locksmithing. When I handed them back, he handed me a business card bearing his name, Walter Gazel, and an image of a leaping deer, apparently a clue to ensure correct pronunciation of his name. "You may keep this one," he said and that finally concluded our dance of identifications and allowed a handshake. "Now show me the patients, please."

I led him inside to the two doors that required his attention. The lock of the plain, outer door had been picked and damaged in the process; the lock on the steel-clad inner door had been breached with an explosive which had extensively damaged the door also. After a cursory examination, he returned to his truck and brought in a tool box and then a dolly loaded with a new steel-clad door.

I was dumbfounded that such a small man could handle what was obviously that heavy door, even with a dolly, but he didn't even draw breath as he hefted it. "How do you know that door will fit?" I asked.

"We installed these doors initially and had the dimensions and specifications on file. We had the steel door fabricated as soon as we learned there was a need for it. After I replace the lock and knob on the outer door, I'll just take the damaged inner door off the hinges and hang this new one. I will then give you two sets of keys for the new locks. All in a day's work." Actually he had the doors up and running within the hour and the damaged door loaded on his truck 10 minutes later.

Hobo and I stood by, I watching the masterful way Mr. Gazel went about his work, Hobo on the alert for any threatening move this stranger might make in my direction.

"Now, I'll have a look at that safe." He adjusted his glasses and peered carefully at the engraving on the safe's door. "Aha, this is our model D86. Our files show a modification made by the customer that may have altered the combination. I'll just try the original combination." Which he did from memory, wearing a stethoscope, and intently listening to the tumblers revolving and falling into place inside the door. He played with the dial in various ways, always testing the levers after each group of settings. None of his manipulations opened the door.

At last, he turned to me with a serious look on his face. "Miss Bell, I'm going to give you a lesson in security. Owners of Diebolt combination-lock safes may die and take the combination with them to the grave, or they may write the combination on some medium that is irretrievably lost or destroyed. However, with the proper authorization, the combination is available. For every Diebolt safe, whether it is a small one embedded in a bedroom wall to contain Milady's diamonds or a bank vault storing gold ingots, there is a log securely kept in the Diebolt vaults where the serial number of the safe can be matched to its original combination. I came here with the combination of this safe as it appears in that log. It has become absolutely clear that the original combination has been altered or destroyed. The only way to open this safe is to destroy the locking mechanism or to try each item on a list of a million or more computer-generated random combinations. The first way may cause a serious risk to the contents of the safe; the second way is possible but not practical since it would require months or years to exhaust the list. My report to my masters which they will no doubt convey to Mr. O'Leary will state that this safe cannot be opened other than by destruction of the lock."

His conclusion didn't surprise me. Cousin Willy knew about the secure log and had decided to circumvent the company's precautions. He had altered the combination and only he and Hobo knew the new one. He was dead and Hobo wasn't talking.

"Ah, well," I said. "Then that's that, and your work here is done. Would you care for some refreshment before you leave?"

He refused my offer and bowed ceremoniously to me as he prepared to get in the truck. When he had disappeared down the drive, I called Dan to tell him security of the locked rooms had been restored and that Mr. Willy's secret was still secret. He was philosophical.

"Just means a delay, but a delay isn't all bad. AIM's engineers are poring over the patents and their lawyers are reviewing the licensing agreements. They won't soon come to a stage of the negotiations when we *must* have the safe open. Time enough to have Mr. Gazel back with his nitro or amatol or whatever to blow the lock. So sleep soundly in the meantime."

I did, but Hobo was restless and rose two or three times every night to inspect the downstairs rooms for intruders. I would hear his nails clicking on the floors and then go back to sleep, secure in the knowledge that he was on duty.

The weather turned crisp and the skies turned brilliant blue as September passed into October. Rosy said no more about leaving me for a job elsewhere and I did not broach the subject. Let sleeping dogs lie was my motto. I worked on my translation and sorting Cousin Willy's papers in time I stole from household chores and hikes with Hobo. Deputy Roth had checked in with news of the burglars; a tap on Schell's phone had located Jonas in Miami and Miami police were keeping a close eye on dives and girlfriends he was known to patronize. The FBI had come through with the evidence the district attorney wanted and the deputy assured me that it was only a matter of time before Jonas was picked up. For the time being, the sheriff's department's priority was fire alerts throughout the county. A dry, hot summer had turned extensive areas of forest to tinder. Hobo and I were well aware of the conditions. Our walks raised a fine dust from dried-out leaf mold and often set us to sneezing and coughing. But all in all, other than the fire threat, things were going pretty well, I thought.

Hobo seemed restless lately; I often woke to hear his nails clicking on the floors during the night. I attributed his unease to the number of strangers recently in the house and paid no attention to it. Nevertheless one night around 2 A.M. he seemed more agitated than usual. I thought I smelled wood smoke and got up to look out of the window. Craning my neck, I could see a pink glow in the southern sky so I dressed and put on heavy shoes to go downstairs. From the back veranda I could see a line of flames twinkling along the Baker lands that fronted on the Corona road. The threat of fire had been realized! A light wind carried a smell of smoke that was gradually growing stronger.

When I phoned Eugenia, she answered on the first ring. "I know, I know, and I'm keeping an eye on things. I called 9-1-1 and the dispatcher told me a crew of firefighters were working a minor blaze along the road. The only thing I have to worry about is for the wind to strengthen and shift from the south to the west. That happened years ago when I was a child and a fire came raging up the ravine and burned up the Millman house. It could happen again but the only thing I can do about it is pray for rain."

"Eugenia, if the wind shifts you'll be in danger. Can you make it over here? Bald Knob is safe so far."

"I'd rather wait until daylight. That path is tricky in the dark and the danger isn't acute as yet. I'll keep you posted."

I stayed on the back veranda, cell phone in hand. By four o'clock the wind from the south had freshened and the line of flames began to extend across the lower reaches of Hudson Road just east of Corona. I got out the binoculars and in the morning murk I thought I could make out steam rising above the roofs of Corona. The folks of the town must be hosing down flames menacing outlying houses. Eugenia called to tell me she was still OK but on the alert. Hobo was with me on the veranda but pacing nervously back and forth, only stopping long enough to shove his muzzle into my hand from time to time. He was either reassuring himself or me, I wasn't sure.

By five o'clock the line of flames, still obeying that south wind, had crossed the lower part of the Bell lands and paralleling the Corona road, had headed onto Andy's land. If the wind shifted to blow from the west, the flames would not only rush up the Baker ravine, they would also imperil the houses on Barber Road which led east from the Corona road, Andy's cottage among them. I called him but got no answer. I inferred he was out watching the fire on the move or preparing to fight it if it got too close to his house.

By six o'clock the lower woods on the Bell land were alight as much as a quarter mile from the Corona road. I could hear the fire crackling and hissing as it ran through the underbrush; it seemed to move too fast to torch the mature trees. Although the lower segment of Hudson Road now had to be impassable, the up-slopes below Bald Knob were still unscathed. I waked Rosy to inform her of developments. She concealed her worry with a wisecrack—in her opinion Hudson Road didn't need a holocaust to be Hell. Eugenia called again and told me she was starting for Bald Knob because the wind was now coming strongly from the west. Flames were starting up the ravine and moving fast. I set out to meet her under a lurid sky where the sun struggled to penetrate the smoke clouds born as the green foliage in the ravine took fire. Eugenia lugged a little suitcase as she moved along the trail at a deliberate pace. I took the suitcase from her for the last half of the distance. When we reached the Bell house, Rosy had made coffee and had pancake batter ready for the griddle. I made one more observation of the lower areas of the Bell land and tried Andy's phone one more time before we sat down to eat. I was beginning to worry about Andy but without hearing from him, worry was fruitless.

Andy called at seven; his cottage was intact and all of the cattle in the lower meadows had been moved to safer areas. He apologized for not getting in touch sooner but he was out working cattle as fast as he could. The fire had taken out two houses on Barber Road but the rest of them survived when the fire encountered a line of bare stone cliffs. He said he was on his way to the Bell house to check on Rosy and me. I told him we had pancakes waiting. Arriving sweaty and smudged with smoke, he happily greeted a tall stack dripping with butter and syrup.

Eugenia was calm but glum, sure that her little homestead was in ruins, victim to the same fate as her childhood home. She recalled, "I was five when my mama snatched me out of bed and wrapped me in a blanket. She carried me through the woods on the Bell-Baker trail while my papa stayed behind to fight the fire. It didn't do any good. He was fillin' pails of water as fast as he could pump it up. My big brothers were carryin' and throwin' them but it was hopeless. When the rain started, it sizzled and steamed on the hot earth and the ashes stunk and the house was gone. The tenant house was only half-burned and papa fixed it up for us to live in but never got the big house rebuilt. It was a sad time but my mama said we should stop cryin' and start praisin' God that all of us was all right. Said it with tears streamin' down her cheeks."

Rosy was patting Eugenia's shoulder and murmuring, "Becca will go over as soon as it's safe and maybe, God willing, everything will have been spared."

The rest of us sat around the table in silence. Nothing much to say.

The day had dawned overcast. Full daylight disclosed a blackened verge along the Corona road as far as we could see to the south and as far as we could see to the north. I called Burr Worman's store for news of the town. I was sure he would be in the store, catering to fire crews and news crews. He reported that the fire had bypassed Corona but just barely. "More people was prayin' than cussin' while they hosed down their houses. Me too! Now the firemen are just keepin' an eye on a few embers a-glowin' here and there. They think it was just good luck that most of the fire stayed on worthless land."

Rosy had turned on the kitchen TV but Burr's news was more up to date. A long-haired bosomy weathergirl was promising rain before the day was over. I trained the binoculars on the Baker woods on the south side of Hudson Road, but saw only the familiar heavy canopy of trees that blocked the view of the house and barn area. Andy thought a picture of events over there called for exploration on foot, and I agreed. Eugenia sat slumped despondently over her coffee. "I can't bear to go," she muttered. "I want to know what's what but…."

Andy interrupted "You don't have to go. There's no smoke rising over there and if Becca will guide me, I'm willing to try the trail." Eugenia's gratitude spilled into pathetic tears. Leaving Rosy to comfort her, Andy, Hobo, and I headed for the Baker homestead.

The trail seemed untouched by the fire for most of its length. Cassandra emerged from the brush at her usual spot to hiss and growl at Hobo but her defiance was significantly less spirited than her wont. When she took up the path to lead us, I could see she was treading carefully as if on tender paws and her coat was disheveled and singed in patches. At first view of Eugenia's tidy little yard, I gasped. Her fears were realized. Everything that had been green was now black and the house was a steaming, smoking ruin. The barn was a partial ruin. The shelves on which she stacked finished work had collapsed and the pots and plates were in tumbled heaps. Many of the pieces seemed still to be whole. The large jars and pots designed for patio planting were mostly intact; since they had been stored on the barn floor where charred rafters still held up the roof, they had not been crushed. My thought was that her pottery had endured fire to become enduring when fired again. The heavy beams that had sheltered the fires of her kiln were in place, scorched but otherwise undamaged. Her wheel was a mass of charred wood and metal parts. Although there were no means to make more pots, and no house to live in, the remaining pots were probably sellable. I suspected she would find little cheer in that news.

Andy and I were obliged to walk carefully through the chaos. The ground was very hot in the immediate vicinity of the destroyed buildings but the forest around the homestead was relatively intact. The stony walls of the ravine had acted like a chimney to capture and funnel flames from the lower blaze and to focus them on the yard and buildings. In spite of the drought, the little stream running through the ravine had nurtured green foliage and brushy growth, but quantities of dead, dry, woody trash accumulated over years were enough to support a fierce fire when given the chance. Now the burnt residue of the living and dead material choked the stream in an unpleasant stinking reek.

Andy and I stood looking at one another, downcast by what we saw and even more by the prospect of having to report to Eugenia. The promised rain began to fall, lightly wetting burnt wood and grass. I remembered Eugenia remembering "it stunk" and it certainly did. Andy and I ducked our heads and started on the trail for Bald Knob. Cassandra ignored Hobo and came to wrap herself purring around my ankles. She must have remembered me rescuing her after she was shot, because she tolerated being picked up and carried. Light rain had grown rather heavy by the time we reached Bald Knob. Andy and I were both soaked and he used it as a cowardly excuse to jump on his ATV without coming into the house.

When I put Cassandra down on the living room floor, she lit out on her sore feet for the kitchen and leaped into Eugenia's lap. Tears Eugenia hadn't so far spent on her worries now joined the raindrops on Cassie's singed and grimy fur. I left them comforting one another and went to change clothes. When I came down again, Cassie was huddled over a bowl of food and Eugenia had recovered her composure. I described to Eugenia what we had found and she nodded dry-eyed. "I thought so," she said. "I'll have to be your boarder if you'll have me. When the weather clears up, perhaps you'll go over with me to take stock of the pots I still have left. They're probably worth something."

Rosy was sniffing and blowing her nose. "I feel so bad. You've lost so much. Have you got any money to tide you over? If not, call on me. It must be terrible to know all your personal papers have gone up in smoke."

That got a chuckle out of Eugenia. "No personal papers or money went up in smoke. I've been prepared for years against some kind of catastrophe. My savings and the deeds and precious papers are as safe and sound as if they were in Willy's monster vault. I'll show you when we go over."

The weather continued to be rainy for the next few days. Rosy and I watched Eugenia carefully for signs of depression but she seemed to be bearing up well. Perhaps it helped that Cassie had remembered from her previous experience at Bald Knob how to live in a house and have regular meals. The cat had even adjusted to Hobo; aside from giving him a wide berth, she ignored him. Because of sharing the litter boxes and mealtimes, Sheba had to make the most adjustments. She had managed her earlier exposure to Cassie by hiding or snuggling with Hobo when Cassie was up and about. But she had since grown in confidence and size and now upon her first encounter with Cassie, with every hair on her body and tail standing on end, she hissed, spat, and swatted her in the face. Having made her point as top cat in the Bell house, she strolled off to begin busily grooming herself. Cassie blinked and bore it. Thereafter, the two cats maintained a cautious truce.

Hobo and I hiked down the lane to Hudson Road and then on to the burnt lands. The weather had remained overcast with occasional light misty rain and Hudson Road was in no worse shape than it ever was. Only the first half-mile from the surviving green belt on the east side of Corona showed signs of fire. The landscape was blackened and some of the brush that had not burned completely remained as leafless black skeletons. The bark of mature trees showed some signs of charring, leaves on drooping limbs were desiccated ghosts of their original shapes. Only a few evergreens had succumbed to the flames and turned into bare greasy poles. Embers in the hollow spaces of long-fallen timber glowed dully. Overall, the burned-over areas were probably the better for their cleansing by fire. Fast-moving flames had cleared trashy brush and Spring would bring dormant vegetation back. I expected the county road crews would be along soon to replace hazard signs on the road, and if they weren't I'd call them. They might not be the most prompt or most efficient organization in the world to *repair* Hudson Road, but they did act responsibly to mark its risks.

We returned to hot drinks and interested inquiries. Rosy nodded her head wisely and said, "I could have told you that road would have made it. The devil's own always does." Eugenia started to say something about grocery deliveries before she remembered she was living on Bald Knob for the duration. She hadn't yet digested the full extent of her losses, but her face grew somber as she corrected herself. I hastened to say how pleased I was she was staying with us; the question of spending the winter away from the Baker place had solved itself. Rosy chimed in, adding that she was looking forward to teaching more of the intricacies of fancy needlepoint to a willing student. I was delighted that no talk of Rosy leaving for another job had raised its ugly head!

It was the first of November before the weather broke and Eugenia and I traveled the Bell-Baker trail. The grim look on her face as we trotted along the familiar ups and downs and zigs and zags gave me considerable concern. She was obviously preparing for the ugliest of scenarios. Stepping out of the forest into the ruin of her homestead, she squared her shoulders and drew a deep breath. Then in a bemused voice, she said, "It's not really so bad, is it? The buildings are gone but they weren't much anyway."

As we walked around, Eugenia's face brightened. She pointed out the garden plot, "If I can borrow your shovel in the early spring, I can get a crop in." She turned to the mess of char and rust that was her wheel, "I can order a new up-to-date wheel on the phone, I remember the number." She was undaunted by the piles of pots and plates, "I'll get Neil Stevens to come up and take them down to Burr's and we'll advertise a big sale." To cap her plans, she added, "I can live in a tent next summer with a camp stove. Look, the privy is still over there in the woods, as good as ever. It's too bad there's no way of getting a house trailer up here but someone will probably be willing to take on the job of building a small house."

I was astounded. This elderly, no *old*, woman facing the wreck of her world was looking forward to rebuilding it!

"Eugenia, you're going to need money in order to start over. Your pots won't bring in enough..."

She interrupted me, took me by the hand, and led me over to the foot of a hundred-year-old oak tree. "If I had a shovel right now, I could open my cache and find whatever I need to begin again."

My amazement grew. I burst into laughter,

"You are a wonder. It explains why you and Cousin Willy were such close friends. The two of you were cut from the same cloth—tenacious, inventive, tough-minded! I salute you!"

She joined my laughter. "No sense crying. The next time we come over, we'll bring a shovel. I have some digging to do before the ground freezes."

Two days later, the sun was shining, and we did bring a shovel, two in fact. We both dug to unearth a large black pot. Eugenia had brought along a long, strong knife with which she lifted off a wooden stopper set in a wax seal.

"I'm going to empty this for the last time and put the stuff in a bank. Maybe you'll take me to Greenwood sometime and I'll sign up for a safety deposit box and checking and savings accounts. Time for me to enter the twenty second century."

She pulled a plastic grocery bag from her coat pocket and began to take out bundles of currency and thick brown envelopes tied up with string from the jar and stuff them in her bag. The last item she removed was the little wooden box the police had recovered after the Patriot Guard burglars had stolen and pawned her mother's jewelry.

"There now," she said, "I'll just put the lid on again and cover this up. I don't expect to use it again but it may come in handy some time."

We stopped on the trail back to Bald Knob to sit down for a few minutes. Eugenia broke the silence. "You have become like a daughter to me. I love you for everything you do for me. I won't insult you by offering to pay for my room and board at Bald Knob but I do intend to change my will to acknowledge your kindness."

I tried to interrupt but she put her hand on my wrist to stop me. "As soon as I get to Greenwood and a lawyer, I intend to make you the trustee of the Baker lands, the whole 800 acres that will be a wildlife preserve. The trustee will receive a salary, a mere pittance compared to what Willy dealt out, but it won't be tied up in any crazy scheme. It'll be free and clear for you to live on wherever and however you want, with or without Hobo. So there! OK?"

What could I do but hug her and kiss her wrinkled brown cheek. I had no words and when we rose to continue on the trail, I was thinking how much grief collecting on *that* inheritance would cost me. But when it had to be, I promised myself to raise a memorial to this gutsy old woman at the entrance to her wildlife preserve.

The next week was devoted to settling Eugenia's affairs. She and I went to Greenwood for her to make her banking and legal arrangements. While there, we considered replenishing her wardrobe; her little suitcase had held only two dresses, a couple sets of underwear, a nightgown, and a bathrobe. She was appalled at the clothing on display in the stores. She was adamant that she was not about to show her legs in short skirts or her butt in tight pants! Modern was all right but not skimpy or showoffy! She hadn't worn brassieres ever in her life and didn't mean to start. After much reviewing of available lingerie stocks, we found tank tops and leggy underpants that she would tolerate. Acceptable offerings in the shoe store included lace-up sneakers and sturdy oxfords. We returned home with a limited array of purchases and a lot of disappointment. She had always ordered underclothing and men's work-shoes in the past from a tattered Sears catalog at Burr Worman's store. She couldn't understand why things she preferred and was accustomed to weren't carried in stores these days.

Rosy took her in hand and had me call up offerings on-line but nothing met her criteria for both comfort and propriety. In desperation Rosy proposed *making* the kind of clothes she wanted, all it would take was a sewing machine, fabrics, and a few notions. To Eugenia's plaint that we didn't have a sewing machine and she had never sewed in her life other than darning and mending, I proposed the purchase of a machine, patterns, material, *et cetera*, for some dresses. I volunteered Rosy to teach Eugenia how-to. Rosy was willing and blunt, "Any woman that can learn to do such nice needlework, can learn how to sew!" Eugenia gave in, so she and Rosy and I together made a trip to Greenwood. Rosy traveled Hudson Road with her eyes closed and her teeth clenched, but knew exactly the best sewing machine and materials to purchase. We returned home with everything needful for a winter of handiwork and Eugenia's room was turned into a seamstress's workroom. Cousin Willy's decisions for a full length mirror, built-in ironing board, and steam iron in each bedroom's walk-in closet were paying off handsomely.

The household hummed with both Eugenia and Rosy happily engaged in sewing, cooking, and cleaning while I hiked with Hobo, worked on my translation, and continued to rummage through Cousin Willy's documentations. One evening after everyone else had retired, I returned to his folder of correspondence with the Diebolt people. As I picked it up, I pushed aside the folder documenting Hobo's parentage; it fell open and the scrap of paper with the reading of Hobo's extra chip fell out. Suddenly "R10B35R65B3" looked a lot like a combination! Did Willy's joke about asking Hobo mean the chip under Hobo's skin was the key to opening the safe? It was worth a try. With the keys to Willy's file room and the scribbled paper in hand I went to the room. I held my breath as I tried my hunch.

Using the logic that B in the number probably stood for L, I whipped the dial around right to 10, left to 35, right again to 65, and left to 3, passing zero each time I moved it. I heard some clicks but the levers didn't yield to my hand. I tried a repeat. Perhaps I had not landed full on the numbers. Still no luck. Then I decided to try a variation. Willy should have been called Wily, he loved a puzzle. What if he meant—Right to 10 on the dial, then Back 35 *divisions*, including zero in the count to make 36, then Right to 65 *divisions*, including zero in the count to make 66, and Back 10 *divisions*, including zero in the count to make 11. This time the clicks came rattling along loud and clear and the levers yielded to my grasp! The heavy door swung open and there was the inside of the safe, folders and miniature models of devices arranged on its shelves. Quickly, I closed the safe again. I was so surprised at my success that I doubted my success. So I whirled the dial around several times, and starting from zero, tried my reasoning again. Again the door opened.

I drew a breath of relief. Cousin Willy's safe would not have to be wrecked to find whatever AIM would need to close a deal. I felt good about that. As Cousin Willy's designated caretaker of the house on Bald Knob, I felt responsible for keeping his most private things the way he left them. Now I had to decide whether to tell Dan I had the safe open before opening it had become urgent or to wait until he told me the deadline had arrived and he was calling Mr. Gazel with his drill. I rather relished the idea of keeping the secret until I could surprise Dan at the 11th hour. I decided Cousin Willy's preference would be the latter. I would honor his memory and wait.

We were having Andy to dinner. Eugenia had completed her first dress, a soft blue light-weight wool with long sleeves, a full skirt, and a white collar. She and Rosy wanted to show it off. I had seen it during the process but the final opus was yet to be revealed. The nature of the revelation had been conveyed to Andy; he arrived bearing a corsage of gardenias that he had gone to Greenwood to acquire. First he told Eugenia how beautiful she looked, and how well made her new dress was, and then he handed her the corsage. She was so touched she cried. Andy blushed like a teenager when she grabbed him and kissed him on the mouth.

Thanksgiving came and we celebrated *en famille*, good food and good conversation in equal measure. The weather stayed mild although leaves drifted down in vast quantities. Hobo and I shuffled along the paths, sending many a small creature scurrying. There seemed to be a Lord's plenty of mice and ground squirrels this year. Cassandra had adapted more or less to indoor living, although from time to time she succumbed to wanderlust and scooted out the door between my and Hobo's feet. She always returned in time for the next meal sometimes with undesirable prizes, mousy offerings which she would lay by the veranda door and if given the chance, inside the door. I was amazed that she could catch prey with only the claws of her surviving foreleg, but she had undoubtedly adapted. The proof lay in the success of her catches. She responded to Eugenia's scolding with a wide-eyed stare, a picture of innocence. Sheba looked over the mouse crop with a dainty sniff but not one mouse was ever devoured by either cat.

One morning, a dreary day with rain pouring over the autumnal landscape, I announced at breakfast that I intended to spend the day exploring in some detail the locked rooms of the first floor. Now that I had solved the secret of Cousin Willy's safe (so far the secret remained only mine and Hobo's), I felt entitled to rummage his file- and work-rooms.

Eugenia encouraged me. "It's about time! I'm sure Willy, wherever the old reprobate is, wonders why you've waited so long to think about it. Like the typical old bachelor he was, he thought women and curiosity were two sides of a coin." When I explained my diffidence, she snorted, "Hogwash! He wouldn't have entrusted his treasures to you if he hadn't intended for you to look them over and admire them."

But as I tried to familiarize myself with his treasures, I had to admit I was incompetent to appreciate them. Mechanical and industrial matters were so far from my experience that all I could do was to look and wonder at their complications. The outer room that I called the file room featured a bank of gray metal file cabinets in the center of the room. They held folders of business documents—records I presumed of patent applications and licensing agreements. Some unusual cabinets along the wall had pull-out drawers, 36 inches wide and 36 inches deep, which contained rolls of heavy paper tagged with cryptic labels and tied with blue ribbons. They reminded me of scrolls I had seen in the scriptorium of a European monastery. The ribbon had broken on one roll, disclosing drawings that in my ignorance I called blueprints. Kitchen-style cabinets with paneled doors covered the walls from floor to ceiling. I needed the kitchen ladder to look into those on the upper level—a lot of models, some apparently incomplete, residua of failed ideas.

I had given the inner room, the work room as I called it, no more than a cursory glance when Andy first showed it to me. I had noticed the unusual lighting and the drafting tables, but now I looked closely at the little machines that I had at first taken for toys. I know less than nothing about wood- or metal-working machines but one of the tools looked like a lathe and another like a saw. A deep bin contained metal and wood shavings that Cousin Willy apparently had not had time to dump. Drawers in the tables held small delicate hand tools: screw drivers; rasps; calipers, and so on. I was aware that all of his tools were miniaturized versions of full-size equipment, rather like what I imagined a jeweler might use. I could imagine Willy bent intently over some model he was working to bring to completion, no doubt to try out its feasibility in full scale. A few meticulously detailed models stood on shelves. I had not the faintest idea of the applicability of these inventions but I could appreciate the elegance of the models and the skill and effort that went into them.

I gave up trying to understand the contents of the file- and work-room. If negotiations with AIM should come to a head, time enough to turn the whole problem over to O'Leary. For the time being, I locked up the rooms again and turned my time and attention to translating *Les Miserables*. I had just arrived at Hugo's telling of Waterloo. Monsieur Lemaire, my instructor for French history at the Sorbonne, was elderly, with flyaway gray hair, big ears, and a rabbity face. In line with his passion for the Napoleonic saga, he assigned me a map and Hugo's description of the terrain and military movements of what came to be called the Battle of Waterloo. "Read it, walk it, live it!" he ordered, his eyes flashing behind the lenses of his glasses. "Then you will understand what it means to France." My old enthusiasm rekindled as I worked on this phase of my translation. My heart beat fast, my fingers raced over the keyboard, and I forgot to eat.

I really loved the task. It not only utilized my linguistic expertise and French vocabulary, it also exercised my knowledge of the English language. I sometimes spent a half day on the best wording of a paragraph only to set it aside for another go later. I stood in awe of Hugo's command of the storytelling craft, and I was resolved to do it credit in my choices of English words and phrases.

Time passed profitably and happily at the Bell homestead. Rosy and Eugenia's friendship continued to flourish. They were never bored with one another's company because there were recipes to discuss and execute, new clothes to plan and sew, needlepoint patterns to work out, and TV programs to discuss. Cassandra and Sheba had come to a peaceable accommodation. Hobo's devotion to me never flagged and even started to extend to the other members of the household. All of the relationships in my vicinity seemed to be in order except one. I thought again as I so often had what a great family I had and how indebted I was to Cousin Willy for making it happen. My happiness had all come about from making my way that first time through the hardships of Hudson Road to Bald Knob and deciding to take up Cousin Willy's challenge. I had it all, a family of friends, human and animal. I needed nothing more and I asked for nothing more, only that it would last. The thought crossed my mind and was quickly dismissed that there *was* something more but....

A moderately heavy snowfall gave us a white Christmas but we had prepared for isolation with a good supply of holiday viands. We celebrated Christmas Day with feasting, wine, and song. Gifts were homemade, handmade, and delightful. Eugenia had recently learned to knit and Rosy, Andy, and I received long, warm, woolly scarves. Rosy had sewed Christmas stockings decorated with stars and steeples. She said it was a pleasure to honor the Christian tradition. In the years of her marriage to Izzy, Hanukkah celebrations never seemed to measure up to her childhood memories of Christmas. Andy brought over a quarter of beef, cut up and packaged for the freezer. Eugenia, with a straight face and a twinkle in her eye, joked, saying when she was a girl, the only time her family had this much beef on hand was when a cow died. Andy with an equally serious mien offered to take it back and put it in his freezer. "Over my dead body," Eugenia cried, "I'm already planning the roasts and chops."

In January Dan O'Leary phoned to tell me that the negotiations with AIM were heating up and questions were arising about those of Willy's inventions not yet patented. Dan was about to call Diebolt and have them send Mr. Gazel to break into the safe.

"Don't!" I exclaimed.

He was puzzled. "What have you found?"

"What you have to see before sealing a deal with AIM!" I replied.

I rather begrudged giving up a dramatic revelation of my news standing at the site. But I realized that was silly and I spilled my surprise in one breathless rush. "I got the safe open and I think you should bring an engineer who can evaluate what's in it. Just so you know the position from which you can or will negotiate the final deal."

"Got the safe open! How? What did you use? A magic wand? Fairy dust? I can hardly believe this. Gazel was so positive that the lock was forever frozen."

"I found the combination with which Cousin Willy replaced the original one. It's quite a story and I'm not prepared to tell it until you come and see that it works. I looked inside when I had it open. But other than some models and some documents, I don't know what I saw. It will take an engineer to evaluate them."

Dan was jubilant. He had experts on standby. How soon could he bring them to Bald Knob? When I proposed the coming weekend, he committed to a two-day stay after arrival at 11 A.M. Friday, weather permitting. I couldn't wait to sign off so I could get my household in gear to prepare for the visit. But Dan was all agog over the disclosure of the mystery contents of the safe. He babbled on about renting a Land Rover for the trip up Hudson Road, just to make sure that he and his colleagues arrived alive. I wondered what kind of survival gear our guests were planning but expected red wool plaid caps and jackets.

Eugenia and Rosy were delighted with the prospect of company and launched into a frenzy of baking and freezing. I was not enlisted except to go to the Greenwood A&P for the constituents of a variety of casseroles. My job was to refresh the bed and bathroom linens. The weather held and the guests arrived on schedule, unscathed by their journey. Introductions took place on the veranda. Dan had brought two eminent engineers: Thomas G. Cromwell, Ph.D., Chair of the Engineering Department at Purdue; and Oliver DeBeers Harrison, Ph.D. Emeritus, Carnegie Mellon Institute, a much-published author of articles in engineering journals. Cromwell was tall, skinny, and laconic; he was togged out in a flannel shirt, corduroy pants, heavy boots, and a cap adorned with a Boilermaker logo. Harrison was short, fat, red-faced, and talkative; he wore Carhart overalls and a floppy-brimmed felt hat, both rather the worse for wear. I led the guests to their rooms, allowed them time to freshen up, then sat them down to a lunch that was both hearty and light. Rosy's menu was contrived to keep the men awake for serious business in the afternoon. Andy arrived while we were eating. I thought his longtime and faithful attention to security of Cousin Willy's affairs deserved to be in on the impending opening of the safe.

After lunch, dangling my impressive key ring, I led the guests to the secret rooms and showed them briefly around. Cromwell nodded quiet approval of the arrangements. Harrison's approval was vocal; he put Cousin Willy's layout on a par with Edison's Menlo Park. I thought his effusions were overkill when I remembered photos I had seen of the Menlo Park establishment, but I charged them up to Harrison's background as an author.

I then did my magic with the combination of the safe and proposed leaving the experts to their deliberations. Dan, I thought, was a little disappointed that there were no fireworks as the safe's door swung back. The experts were eager to get started on their examinations. Andy watched politely noncommittal. I had a feeling that the contents of the safe were no surprise to him.

I played hostess. "Gentlemen, the premises are at your disposal. Coffee, tea, and soda are available in the kitchen and the powder room is the first door on the right in the hall. Dinner is planned for 6:30 P.M. I will lock up the safe and these rooms again at 6 and reopen them at whatever hour you would like tomorrow morning. Make yourselves at home. If you need anything, just ask. OK?"

Andy and I left Dan and his experts to go about whatever they were going to do. I settled down in my office and Andy joined me. We turned TV on to a classic movie presentation, put up our feet, and relaxed. It wasn't long before Dan came in.

"Anything I would do around those guys would only hinder them. They are as happy as kids in a candy store. I'm going to grab a cup of coffee and then I want to be told how you solved the mystery of the safe."

Andy looked at me and said, "Me, too."

I began my tale by reminding Andy of his words when I came to Bald Knob the first time. "You told me the safe held the drawings for Willy's most valuable inventions and only he and Hobo knew the combination. At the moment, I didn't care that only Hobo was left to know it. I didn't see then any need to open the safe. Later, as I looked through Mr. Willy's journals and desk files to see what I might learn about my own origins, in the back of my mind I did wonder about the lost combination. I asked you, Dan, if you had any record of it and you said no, but there was no urgency for finding it.

"There was some evidence from Hankins's tries to get in the house that the contents of the locked rooms and the safe had considerable commercial value but when he backed off, I put the inaccessibility of the safe out of my mind. The armed burglars brought a new dimension to the mystery."

"Yes," Dan said, "but we soon learned that their interest wasn't industrial espionage. However, about that time AIM's interest in the 'Bell Legacy' heated up and I was obliged to consider the mystery of the safe important to negotiations to sell the legacy."

I took up the tale again, "All along I, as tenant of the Bell homestead, was worried by attempts of persons of ill intent trying to broach our simple forms of security. Then came the foiled burglary and Hobo was shot and wounded. In my joy over his survival, I wanted to lavish affection on him. I spent my caresses on the nape of his neck in order to avoid his wounds. I knew he probably had an i.d. chip under the skin there, almost all cherished pets do. But Hobo had *two*. The vet explained that one chip was the standard chip recorded for the national pet registry and the other was a chip Mr. Willy had given him to insert. Before I took Hobo home that day, the vet scanned both chips with his detector wand and I scribbled the

138

separate readings on a scrap of paper that I brought home and then forgot about among the papers on my desk. This is the scrap of paper. Notice the two sets of numbers. The one with the dots is the national registry number."

"I don't want to blow your surprise, but I'm willing to bet that this scrap of paper played a part in solving the mystery of the safe." Dan blurted out and Andy nodded in agreement.

"Correct! But the whole clue depended on a coincidence. I was still rummaging through the files in this desk. I happened to have these two file folders out at the same time and read them almost concurrently. The correspondence with the Diebolt safe company led me to believe Cousin Willy had customized the combination of the safe."

I handed the Diebolt letters to Andy and Dan. "But the letters only told me what Mr. Gazel would confirm. The original combination on file with the maker wasn't going to work and the only way to gain access was to blow up the lock. The papers documenting Hobo's acquisition gave me a ballpark date for the vet's workup in which the chips had been inserted; that date was pretty close to the dates on the Diebolt correspondence. There was nothing explicit to confer special importance to Hobo's extra chip. Until Hobo was injured, only the vet had seen the reading on the chip and casual consideration of the reading was just so much gobble-de-gook to him and to me. At the vet's suggestion I scribbled the readings of the chips on a scrap of paper and took the paper home with me. Weeks later I found the scrap of paper and decided it should be filed with Hobo's documents.

"Then just before Thanksgiving I was getting the mess on my desk straightened out and putting file folders back in the drawer. When I picked up Hobo's file, the scrap of paper with the readings fell out. The registration chip showed 9 numbers in 3 sets, three digits each set, and the sets separated by dots. The reading of the extra chip was jumble of numbers and letters. As I looked at it, various clues came together in my mind and I saw the jumble looking a lot like a combination. I remembered Willy's aggravation at Diebolt's dismissal of his proposal. So I inferred that he had made a spiteful gesture and put his new combination for the safe on a chip that he had the vet to insert under Hobo's hide. I went to the safe and after taking into account Mr. Willy's devious ways, came up a winner. I was glad that the safe wouldn't have to be breached by force to check its contents. I wanted to protect Cousin Willy's privacy until it absolutely had to be breached. There seemed to be no imminent need to explore the contents, so I just sat on what I had learned. Then you, Dan, told me the negotiations with AIM had gone critical you needed to know what was in the mystery safe. So I told you I could get the safe open without destroying the lock. Now here you are, waiting for the report of the experts. End of story."

Just then Harrison appeared in the door. "Can you provide a pad of paper and a pencil? Tom and I want to make some notes for our reports to Dan. As of the moment we are in agreement on the remarkable value of the stuff in the safe but we differ on some minor aspects. The other material is valuable but not world-shaking."

Dan jumped up and followed Harrison back to the scene of the examinations. Andy grinned as he rose and stretched. Turning to me, he said,

"Mr. Willy would be proud of you. 'A real Bell' he would say. You figured out his trick but kept your counsel until it mattered."

I felt deflated, like a limp balloon. Tension over. The burden of responsibility for the Bell legacy was about to be lifted from me. When I recovered from this day, I would be ready to dance in the streets, providing Hudson Road were redefined as a street and the county ever got it fit for dancing. Seeing Andy's gleeful expression, I got up, threw my arms around him, and planted a big kiss right on his mouth. I was surprised and shocked at his reaction. There was passion in his response, passion I had never suspected. I thought we were just good friends. I pulled away to get time and distance enough to think about what had just happened.

At this moment, Eugenia popped in the door. "Rosy and I figured Andy would be here to dine with us. We think the table can seat seven as easily as six, and Rosy thinks we can lay out the food buffet style on the kitchen counters. Andy, please come look over the menu and decide what wines to bring up."

Just as quickly she popped back out. Andy and I smiled shyly at one another and we got busy on the arrangements for a gala dinner. Hobo was caught up in the spirit of celebration and gamboled gaily in front of us as we walked out to the kitchen.

Dan called on March 27th to announce that AIM's people and trucks would arrive on April 1 to pack the Bell legacy and cart it off to their headquarters in Marion.

"I'll welcome them with open arms. Are any of them staying over?"

Dan chuckled. "I made it plain that they were on their own but if they wanted to pitch a tent and put up a Port-o-Let out by the barn, they were free to do so. I think your only commitment is to keep them from banging up your woodwork as they move the stuff out of the locked rooms. Todd Morgan, the CEO, will come and first of all remove and carry off the contents of the safe. After that the underlings will follow through on the less sensitive stuff."

Trying not to sound too jubilant, I reminded Dan that it would be three years to the day since I had his letter announcing my kinsman's legacy. "It's been an eventful three years. I haven't regretted my decision to sign that contract but I'll be happy to be relieved of responsibility for such valuable property as Cousin Willy left in his locked rooms. I have plans to clear out those rooms and do them up for some useful purpose. What do you think of tasteful drapery around the safe? Then household furniture, we really need a dining room."

Dan burst into a prolonged gale of hearty laughter. When he had caught his breath again, he shared major news. "What was in that safe added eighty million dollars to what AIM was willing originally to pay the trust. After Todd had read Cromwell's and Harrison's reports of the devices Mr. Bell proposed for development, he was starry-eyed with plans to work up applications to solar and wind power. The whole amount will be paid the trust in installments over a period of 10 years. AIM's stock has just jumped 15 points based on rumor alone. I want you know, Rebecca, your stewardship of the Bell legacy was not merely commendable, it was outstanding and highly profitable."

"Hobo and I thank you for your kind words. When will we see you again?"

Not for a while, he said. The trust's business had taken up so much of his time, that he needed to catch up on the firm's work. I didn't let on but I found the prospect of benign neglect a relief from the hustle and bustle we had endured with all our company. The household would be happy to fall back into its sleepy ways. Eugenia was deep in plans to pitch a tent on her home place, install a new potter's wheel, and work on some new stock. I wasn't entirely comfortable with that but how do you curb a headstrong old woman who has had her own way for 60 years or more. I opted not to try.

Rosy tried to talk Eugenia out of her plan, especially when she learned Eugenia would be chopping wood to fuel her kiln. When her lectures got her nowhere with Eugenia, she turned to me. "Talk to her! That's too hard a work for a woman her age. She'll kill herself, have a heart attack, or cut her leg off with the axe." When I said I planned to get Eugenia a cell phone and insist she wear it all the time, Rosy was partially pacified, but not convinced. "She'll forget she has it and she'll hurt herself and never a peep out of her. Besides how's she gonna charge it?" Rosy didn't give up trying, even when I told her the power company had restored electrical service to the remaining barn structure.

On April 1, a convoy of white panel trucks decked out with AIM's logo came up Hudson Road and the lane, and parked themselves neatly next to the veranda. A nice young man, his coveralls adorned with a patch depicting AIM's logo (an arrow lofting steeply toward a sunlit cloud), introduced himself as "Ron" and asked to be shown into the locked rooms. As I let him in, I noticed drivers of the parked trucks taking out and setting up a portable privy. I swallowed a giggle just in time. As they finished, a Land Rover arrived and Todd Morgan jumped out and introduced himself. A fellow in his mid-thirties, he was prematurely gray but his physique was superbly fit. He took out of his vehicle a steel box the size of a foot locker and with me in the lead, entered to empty the safe. I opened it for him and watched him remove and carefully pack the contents in his steel box. Bidding me good-bye and thanks, he returned to his Rover and drove off.

The "underlings," as Dan had called them, then took over and I left them undisturbed at their task.

Hobo was nervous. All those strangers! But he stuck close to me and remembered his manners. The first team carried in a huge bundle of tissue paper and a tool box. The first thing in the outer room to go was the central bank of file cabinets. Dismantled, it filled two trucks which immediately took off for their destination. The next thing was the blueprint cabinet. Its awkward size posed something of a problem to load and I heard some muffled oaths before that truck was ready to leave. Now the tissue paper came into play. Each model was taken down from the cabinet, carefully wrapped in tissue paper, and placed tenderly in a plastic crate. The crates were carried out, filling three trucks—and it was 6 P.M. and twilight setting in. Ron came in and asked my permission to stay in the parking area for the night.

"How are you going to eat and where will you sleep?" I asked.

"We have picnic packages and we'll sleep in the empty trucks. If we may, we would like to use your hose to wash up. But if we could bother you for some hot water….?"

Of course, I said. Rosy started to fill stew pots and the tea kettle to boil water which was then taken out to make instant coffee, tea, and hot chocolate at the tailgate of one of the trucks. The men chatted quietly over their food and drink and soon after stretched out in the backs of the three trucks remaining empty. The next morning at first light, I heard splashes and smothered yelps as the men washed up in icy water. I went down and put the stew pots and tea kettle on for boiling water. The weather was clear but nippy and the men welcomed hot drinks. Ron accosted me to say that they were likely to finish loading by noon. They would need another hour to clean the empty rooms and package up trash. I was surprised but the young man said cleanup was covered in the sales contract. I didn't argue. The men went about finishing up; by noon they had emptied all the shelves and cabinets and were packing up their portable privy. Then all but one truck left and the men still on the premises tackled the cleaning with buckets, mops, and rags. Ron asked me to inspect their work, thanked us for the hot water, and took off with the rest of the crew a few minutes after 1 P.M.

Hobo and I retired to my office and collapsed in utter relaxation. Sheba wandered in and climbed in my lap to join me in a long nap. Rosy peeked in at 5 P.M. and asked what I would like for supper. When I said nothing, she got all fussed, thinking I was not feeling well. For her, not eating when one was not ill was tantamount to suicide. I finally convinced her I was not eating because I simply didn't want to make the effort. I heard her in the kitchen telling Eugenia how unwell I was. Eugenia's answer, which carried clearly down the hall, was "She's OK, like a woman who has just delivered a child. Feeling so relieved of her burden that she just wants to shut her eyes and forget."

One sunny morning a week after the grand removal, Rosy and Eugenia took advantage of a 70-degree day to go over to the Baker home site. It was Eugenia's intent to survey and plan how she could get back home, and Rosy's intent to dissuade her every effort. Cassie had decided to prowl the barn for small prey. Hobo, Sheba, and I were alone in the house, I had sat down to work on my translation but I was finding it difficult to keep my mind on my desktop. The memory of that passionate kiss Andy and I had exchanged so recently had been simmering on the back burner of my brain during every moment free from routine concerns.

I was no virgin. But no meaningful commitment had ever blessed, or cursed, me. Now with my thirtieth birthday looming, it was almost inevitable that I would give some thought to a possibility of a permanent relationship. I had gone to dances while I was in high school and college, usually on the arm of a wimp or nerd six inches shorter than myself. I always suspected the invitations were due either as payback for some academic boost I had bestowed on the guy or to the guy's adolescent crush on me. I never worried about the lack of romance, I figured time would roll around and a man my size would appear. In France, I had a torrid three-month affair with a fellow student, a Polish boy Ladislas Kovieski, whose attentions taught me the carnal side of a relationship. But Lad lived on a roller coaster of emotions and I decided long-term companionship with him was too wearing to be practical. Back in Shady Grove, I dated Greg Arnold regularly; he was the six foot six assistant coach of the high school basketball team. We did an every-Saturday-night pizza and movie evening that included a bit of groping on the front seat of his Chevy. I didn't want that connection to go anywhere, Greg was ineffably boring, never had an original thought and talked of nothing but sports. I was incredibly grateful when the newly hired history teacher set her cap for him. Our relationship evaporated and I sent the two of them a very nice wedding gift a few months later.

Thinking back over my encounters I realized I had neither enjoyed nor regretted them. I was busy with my education and later my teaching, and making time for romance had not been high on my agenda. Maybe I had decided to sign the contract with Cousin Willy's estate because I was looking for some adventure, or if not adventure, at least a challenging change from the life that I had already lived. The last three years had certainly provided me with challenges, some of them frightening. But they had given me friends to be cherished and kept close. I didn't know what would happen with Eugenia and Rosy but if my luck held they might be staying close at hand. Nevertheless, one or both of them could leave me any time for life elsewhere. If so, I would still have Hobo's honest and undemanding devotion. *And* there was Andy, *my friend Andy,* since my first day on Bald Knob.

Thinking seriously about my friendship with Andy set me to adding up its plusses. From the first he had been open and helpful; as time passed, he was always *there*, a sounding board for my ideas and whims, a source of dependable and unbiased advice, capable and reliable support to maintain the homestead. Well-educated and well-informed on many points, he had proved to be a great personal companion for an evening of popcorn and a movie, and an impressive and personable dinner guest in the company of lawyers and university professors. He gave Eugenia and Rosy the same kind of respect and deference he gave me. He was kind and considerate to animals, Hobo was his friend, Sheba doted on him. Cassie, well, Cassie was herself but she didn't hiss at him anymore. Then, there was the fact that he was a head taller than me and, when I stopped to take note, very good looking. I realized that I had taken him and his outstanding qualities for granted, that my liking for him had become very nearly loving. That passionate kiss made me think that perhaps he didn't take *me* for granted. But what if I was jumping at an unwarranted conclusion? I didn't want to miss out on an opportunity for grownup love. I was facing a dilemma— did I let Andy know of my feelings for him or did I attempt to get him to voice his feelings for me?

As I sat twiddling a pencil between my fingers and mulling unfamiliar ideas, I heard Andy on the intercom, announcing his entry to check the water softener in the basement. I jumped up to meet him in the hall.

"I was just thinking about you," I said. "I wondered if you would like to join us for dinner. It's my turn to cook. Spaghetti and meatballs."

"You betcha!"

Rosy and Eugenia returned from their survey of the Baker place about 5 o'clock, both of them rather sooty since Rosy had helped Eugenia inventory her marketable pots. Eugenia was euphoric, "I could smell that aroma of spaghetti sauce on the trail, like a thread drawing me along. A great finish to a good day."

"You two have just enough time for a quick soak in your tubs before dinner is ready. Andy is joining us."

Eugenia went upstairs right away but Rosy lingered to favor me with a stage whisper. "That woman is as stubborn as a mule. She's going to kill herself. She'll either die of pneumonia from sleeping in that tent or she'll cut her leg off with the axe. She won't listen to me. Have you talked to her?"

"Yes, but it was wasted breath. She's had her own way for more than 60 years and she's bound to keep on with it. We'll just have to let her alone and see what happens. Now, go relax and get ready for supper."

Rosy made her way upstairs grumbling as Andy came up from the cellar.

"I'm bringing along the dinner wines to go with the gourmet dinner. What's Rosy unhappy about?" he said.

I explained and he laughed. "We'll just have to put up with Eugenia's plans. She won't change them until *she* concludes she has to adjust."

Dinner was a great success, second helpings all around. Rosy's mood improved, due she said to the effect of garlic. "God did good when he made garlic to grow. It cures so many things and tastes good too." Andy left early. He had a cow about to give birth and he expected she might need help. Although I saw him to the door, no goodnight kiss came of it. I told myself that Andy had a sick cow on his mind.

Mulling the quandary I saw in my relationship with Andy, I was also working on renovation of Cousin Willy's workrooms. Dan O'Leary got permission from the trust for me to make major changes to the house, and Ben Bender arranged for an architectural engineer to assess the current structure and plan alterations to meet my wishes. The engineer arrived in a minivan and spent three days poking into every nook and cranny in the house with a camera, a laptop computer, a spiral notebook, and a thing that looked like a gun but was a laser measuring device. He ate lunch and dinner with us and stayed up late in his minivan organizing his data. He was back two weeks later with a huge sheaf of blueprints and cost estimates for the changes I wanted. Much to my relief, Ben was to be in charge of hiring the contractor and letting the bids. The summer promised to be noisy with hammering and sawing, busy with workmen coming and going, air filled by plaster dust and sawdust.

Rosy rolled her eyes and sighed at the prospects. Eugenia was occupied at the Baker place supervising Neil Stevens in setting up her tent and new wheel. She was cooking on a camp stove, her simple fare augmented by Rosy's frequent contributions of what she called "real food." My daily walk with Hobo usually included a stop at the Baker place to leave a pot of stew or thermos of soup and to check on progress. Rosy, having learned the Baker-Bell trail, made frequent visits to assure herself of Eugenia's welfare.

The first work on the Bell house began June 5 with the flooring in Cousin Willy's locked rooms. The contractor had taken down the wall between the hall and the outer room thereby making the large living room even larger. Next the flooring went down in the formerly locked rooms. I had selected a laminate that would cover the concrete floor with an acceptable imitation of the broad plank floors characteristic of the original log cabin. A wall then went up in the outer room to conceal the safe and provide a nice little storage room opposite it. This change created a small hall leading to the inner room which was now defined as the new office and given privacy with a handsome glass-paneled door. Next, windows were cut through the front walls and fitted to provide natural light to both rooms. The fortified window in the inner room was restored to a conventional style. Defining the inner room as the new office brought electricians swarming in to run wiring for the TV, computer, and accessories. By the middle of July, painting of the new rooms was completed and we were ready to move Cousin Willy's office furniture to the new space. At first the huge antique desk seemed to pose a problem, but when one of the carpenters figured out that it was designed for disassembly into two pedestals and the desktop, it was soon moved and reassembled in the new office. The other furniture followed and work started on the old office preliminary to opening it to the kitchen's eat-in area.

I was in the new office fine-tuning the placement of chairs and credenzas when Mr. Blair, the boss carpenter, burst into the room without knocking. Hobo, who was sprawled comfortably on the floor, leaped to his feet, hackles raised and a menacing growl in his throat. Mr. Blair froze, his face ashen. I hastened to reassure him. "It's OK. You startled us. Peace, Hobo, sit and stay."

When his face regained its normal color, Blair said, "Miss Bell, you got to come look at what we found. We'll need you to tell us what to do next."

I followed him to the old office where the carpenters had started to remove the fine walnut paneling. We were saving it for future use and it was being taken down to allow the opening of this room, destined for a formal dining room, into the kitchen. One of the crew simply pointed to a partly freed panel and Blair announced, "It's a secret door. We found the latch when we pulled the panel off the wall. What do we do now?"

"Take it off and let's see what's behind it." More of Cousin Willy's tricks, I thought; he's used the structure supporting the stair to the second floor for a hidey hole. I jumped as the workman yelled, "Hey, there's a trapdoor here." Of course, everyone crowded to look. But because the area was too dark to see much, I got the battery lantern we kept for emergencies from the kitchen cupboard. Then we could see that a door about three feet square had been worked into the floor. I asked the men to open it. It was very heavy but they discovered a handle that engaged with a hook on the bottom of a stair tread.

The trap door covered a cavity, clean and bone dry, about three feet on a side and three feet deep, cut in the living rock of Bald Knob, and containing a chest the dimensions of which were just an inch or so smaller than the hole. In spite of the snug fit, one of the workmen—grunting, panting, and squirming on his belly—managed to extract the chest and set it down in front of me. An image of a bell carved on the lid bore a W in tarnished metal. When I went to open the lid, the straps closing it were pliable and came easily out of the buckles. Inside I found packets of papers tied neatly with twine. Without breaking into the packets, I couldn't identify the papers but they seemed to be family records, letters, and such. What caught my eye particularly was a book bound in blue linen and with AMANDA BELL HER BOOK stamped in gold on the front cover; I knew it instantly as treasure trove for my reading at leisure. The chest and its contents would find its new resting place in Cousin Willy's monumental safe. I asked Blair to carry the chest to the new office and told the men to close the cavity and get on with their demolition work. I kept Amanda's book out for a bed book and started on it that very evening.

Just as the carpenter crew knocked off for the day, Rosy returned from the Baker place, carrying a basket filled with beautiful red tomatoes and a few scrawny roasting ears. "The corn is all that's left from the raccoon raid. Cassie hasn't been very good at keeping the wild life out of the garden. By the way, Eugenia asks if she can come over for a night's sleep in a real bed and a bath in a tub. I told her you would call her." She went on into the kitchen and exclaimed over the plastic tarp installed over the start the crew had made on the hole into the former office. I told her I had a chicken and broccoli casserole in the oven for supper. She began at once to get tomatoes sliced and chilled to go with it while I related the find of the afternoon. "Given enough time and renovation maybe all of your Cousin Willy's surprises will be found. It's a good thing the new office is up and running so you can go through the family papers in that chest."

Eugenia arrived the next morning carrying her small suitcase and went straight upstairs for a bath and fresh clothes. I was in the new office when she came down and collapsed with a sigh in the easy chair.

"I'm tired," she said, "I've closed the Baker Pottery until next spring, banked the kiln and oiled and hooded the wheel. Yesterday Neil Stevens came with the bed of his pickup full of loose hay and we loaded all the pieces for him to take to a store called Country Crafts over in Columbia. Mrs. Mac arranged for the store to take the stuff on consignment. I'm leaving the garden for the wild things but maybe you'll go over and dig the sweet potatoes and white potatoes; they'll be ready in two or three weeks. Ought to make maybe four gunny sacks full, carry them to the foot of the lane and then drive your Jeep down to get them. They'll be nice for the winter. I'm asking you to keep me on from now until next spring. I have to admit that my breath comes short and my knees get wobbly. It's time to be where someone can keep track of me. I'll be 90 my next birthday and...."

I interrupted, "I'll take you to the doctor in Greenwood first thing tomorrow morning..."

Her reaction was fast and tart, "Oh, *NO*, you won't. All I need is a rest and I'll be better. When I get worse, I'll tell you I'm ready for a doctor."

This energetic speech had made her short of breath and the finger she shook at me was shaky. I was shocked to learn her age. I had guessed she was in her eighties but 90! Wow!

"I'm going to ask Andy to take down my tent, fold it up, and store it in the barn. You'll have to guide him over on the trail. Now, show me that chest they found in the wall. Just like Willy, wasn't it?"

Mr. Blair had told me that he and his crew wouldn't be back for a week or so, something about a delay for special beam he needed for the next phase of the work. In the meantime I decided we could plan our furniture purchase. I checked out stores in Columbia and Greenwood and coaxed Rosy into accompanying me for shopping. We ended up with a Mission style suite for the new dining room—a long table, eight chairs, a credenza, and a china cabinet. We completed the furnishings with an area rug in a contemporary pattern of pale swirls on a beige background and a new chandelier in keeping with the Mission theme. I remembered that among the glam accessories I had boxed and stored there was set of chunky candleholders, an outsized bowl of brilliantly colored ceramic fruit, and a gilt fish standing on his nose and flaunting a curvaceous tail fin. I had in mind they would add a neat touch to the dining room décor.

For the space formerly Cousin Willy's file room I had ordered transparent movable panels etched in foliage patterns; when pulled shut they made the space a private sitting room. We picked out a sectional sofa in mouse-gray microsuede, two side chairs upholstered in rose-colored damask, a contemporary coffee table, and an area rug in soft grays, greens, and rose. With end tables and lamps, that room was also complete. When Eugenia had come to check on progress, all she could say was "Oh, my! Oh, my! You've done Willy proud!" I wondered if the charm of the new décor was a factor in her decision to come live at Bald Knob.

Delivery men had moved in the new furniture on the heels of the departing construction crews. I was rather glad that Eugenia had been spared construction noise; Rosy and I got her to nap a lot. I hoped she would confide in Rosy the reason for her taking up residence at Bald Knob.

But maybe Rosy would guess and I would be spared the embarrassment of asking.

For the time being, I made reading Cousin Amanda's book my spare time priority. Unlike Willy, she dated her entries and wrote in a very legible and very elegant Spencerian hand. The first entry was "July 4, 1976. Today my country is 200 years old." She recorded random thoughts and comments in date sequence but often left gaps of days or weeks between them. She wrote about homely subjects: the first frost turning the leaves to red and gold; a doe and her fawn rambling across the meadow; a pair of great blue herons nesting by the old mill pond. Now and then she copied out a line or two of poetry that had particularly struck her fancy. One quote was Edna St Vincent Millay burning her candle at both ends; Amanda made a wistful comment, "I wish I could say that." Although she remembered occasionally college days at DePauw, it was obvious to me that almost all of her adult life had been spent on Bald Knob. She often referred to visits by the children, lamenting that they were children no longer and came seldom and stayed only briefly. In the late 1970s and 1980, she noted that Louise's letters sometimes referred to Cousin Wilfred's aberrant behavior and moods. "I think she is beginning to be afraid of him. How sad that is."

On February 4th, 1981, Amanda wrote "Terrible news! Wilfred and Victor dead at one another's hands, Hattie hysterical, sending Louise to Willy and me here, never wants to lay eyes on Louise again. But Willy and I agree we will give Louise a loving haven." In April, Amanda noted Louise sitting mostly "in stony silence, only rouses when Willy is home and insists on a walk to look at spring flowers." On the 12th of July, she wrote, "My heart is breaking. Louise packed a little suitcase and walked down to Corona to catch the bus, said she was leaving and wouldn't tell me where she was going. She said not to worry, she had enough money to see her through the baby's birth and then she would start on a new life somewhere. How cruel life can be! Especially to the innocent." Thereafter, once in a while she would write "No word from L." As time passed, the beautiful script began to deteriorate and the entries became more and more infrequent and made less and less sense. One on January 1987 left no doubt why. An alien hand wrote, "Mr. Bell insists I keep constant watch lest she burn down the house."

Three pages before the last entry, I found an unopened letter inserted snugly between two blank pages: no return address; postmark November 10, Terre Haute, IN; address Mr. William G. Bell. I guessed that the letter had arrived while Cousin Willy was away and Amanda was on her deathbed. Perhaps her companion had placed it where Willy would find it upon his return. I suspected it was from my mother and had no compunction in opening it. I had to wipe away tears to read it:

Dear Cousin Willy,

> *I write to tell you how Rebecca and I are getting along. I recently had a promotion to quality control officer at my work and a nice raise that came with it. Becca is a happy, outgoing child and I wish you could meet her. She is very much like you, very bright and remarkably able to succeed at any endeavor. You would like her. To the despair of her kindergarten teacher, she reads very well and agitates continually to do so in school where it is not in the curriculum for her age. I want to thank you for your loving advice. If I had not kept her, I would have missed out on the pride and joy I have in her. Your and Cousin Amanda's support in a terrible phase of my life gave me the courage and will to endure. So my thanks forever and ever.*

> *Love, Your Loulou*

At the bottom of the page, in crooked childish print: **I LOVE HOBO BECCA**

There had to be a special bond between Cousin Willy and my mother, and another between that child and Hobo. I didn't remember that "happy, outgoing child." All I remembered was the lonely, mopy kid that only laughed when Doug Conrad made funny faces or when Mary sang comic songs. Now I realized how lucky I had been. But for Cousin Willy's advice I wouldn't have existed and for the Conrads I wouldn't have become a reasonably well adjusted adult.

I laid the book aside and sank into a reverie of happy times that I had allowed myself to forget as the years went by: a visit to the zoo, my hand in my mother's; a children's concert, *Peter and the Wolf,* Mary mimicked the animal sounds for me; milk toast in bed with the measles, mother (or was it Mary?) spooning the warm, sweet liquid into my eager mouth. The dream of days past exploded as Rosy flew into the room.

"It's Eugenia. She was taking a nap and I can't wake her. I'm not sure she's breathing. Come, oh, come, quick!

Moments later, I was upstairs hovering over Eugenia's bed, my hand on the pulse silent in her wrist, my ear to her bony chest. Her eyes were open, her gaze fixed on the ceiling; her hands lay loosely by her sides. I wasn't familiar with death but a heart that was still and eyes that failed to see told me life had left her. I was too shocked to weep.

But Rosy wasn't. "She's dead, isn't she? What can we do? What about that CPR thing?" she sobbed. "Can we call 9-1-1? My Izzy died in the hospital with nurses and doctors and machines around. But Eugenia must have just slept away."

I fell to my knees, grief weighing me down. Eugenia's cell phone was on the bedside stand. I picked it up and punched Andy's number. Andy asked if I was sure she was dead and said he was on his way. I choked on the words but I assured him I was sure. When I got to my feet, I saw that Eugenia had spread out papers from her little suitcase on the vanity table—as if she had had a premonition that we would need them. I steered Rosy to a chair and then got out a fresh sheet and covered Eugenia's body. Her face was perfectly serene, the hint of a smile lay on her lips. Random thoughts crossed my mind. While I was finding my past and my lost mothers in Amanda's book, my dear friend was slipping away from life. When Andy's voice rang out on the intercom, I called out for him to come up. He went directly to Eugenia and felt for a pulse in her neck, then gently closed her eyes.

Turning to me, he said in a voice hoarse with emotion, "She's gone. Some time ago. Her body is already cooling."

When I swayed under the force of my emotion, Andy took me in a close embrace. I finally found my footing and cleared my throat to ask, "What do we do next?"

"When I found Mr. Willy, I called the sheriff for instructions. He asked me if Mr. Willy had a doctor, I said I didn't think so, and he said he would call the coroner. Someone in authority had to pronounce the death and issue a death certificate. While I waited for the coroner, I scrambled up to the Baker place to tell Eugenia. She came over here to sit with the body."

"Now that is our sad duty," I said.

Andy continued. "Then my hired hand and I started on a grave. It dug pretty easy because the ground had thawed. When the coroner had done his thing and left a signed death certificate, Eugenia bathed Mr. Willy and we dressed him in a fine suit and tie and wrapped him in a nice quilt. I called Dan O'Leary and told him we would bury him the next day about 10 A.M. and I talked to Burr Worman and asked him to let the folks in Corona know. The next day the weather was cold but the sun was shining brightly. I asked Eugenia about a preacher and she said Willy believed in God but not in a church. So I got a Bible out of the library and we said the Lord's Prayer standing around the grave and I read the Twenty-third Psalm. Then everybody but Eugenia and Dan left and Neil Stevens and I filled in the grave. While Eugenia cleared out the refrigerator and tidied up a bit, Dan told me about Mr. Willy's plan for you. That was the first I knew what Mr. Willy had set up. Dan asked me to keep looking after the place until he had things settled with you. Well, that's about it."

With a melancholy sigh, he pulled the sheet up and smoothed it.

I said, "Arrangements like Willy's would suit Eugenia just fine. Because she has always said she was the last of her family, there's no one to notify except the neighbors and the lawyer who made out her will. His name is probably somewhere in the papers she laid out on the vanity table."

Among the papers was a fat envelope bearing the word TESTAMENT and the return address and phone number of a lawyer in Greenwood. I also found a record copy of a visit a week ago to Dr. Grant (the doctor who had treated her broken leg months ago) and a prescription he had written but which she had not had filled. I called him and he promised to come as soon as he could get away from the office. Rosy had regained a degree of composure so I sent her to make preparations for a light meal while I called Burr Worman and Dan O'Leary. Burr surprised me by choking up but he said he would pass the word in Corona about burial tomorrow afternoon.

Dan expressed condolences but had court commitments for the next two days; he would come to pay his respects on Saturday.

With the phone chores done, I sat quietly watching over the still form on the bed. I was learning that grief drains energy as much as strenuous activity does. As deeply grieved as I was, I didn't intend to cry. I had learned in my mopey childhood that crying never solved anything, and I had never formed the habit. Nevertheless, now slow tears began to roll down my cheeks. Until this moment I had not realized what an anchor this woman had been for me in the peculiar circumstances I encountered on Bald Knob. Her tales of Cousin Willy's sayings and doings had clothed him in flesh and blood; her honest telling of my mother's tragedy had emphasized her courage and love for me. Now those tales coupled with the bits and pieces I had learned from Cousin Amanda's and Cousin Willy's writings had given me a *history*. Granted that history was spotty, it was at the same time true and real and I could be part of it. I knew I wasn't crying for her but for me and how much I would miss her.

Hobo, freed of the usual rules by the unusual situation in the house, had ventured up the stairs to sit by me and put his head in my lap. I smoothed his ears and was grateful for his sympathy.

Dr. Grant arrived about 6 P.M. I stood by as he performed his examination. Sitting at the vanity to fill out the death certificate, he told me, "Her death is no surprise. Last week when I saw her, her heart was very weak. The medication I prescribed was meant to strengthen cardiac efficiency but I see she failed to have the prescription filled. She was a person of character, strong-willed and determined to face death on her own terms. You have my sympathy for her loss. She spoke most kindly of you." He continued in a businesslike tone, "I'll take care of registering the death certificate tomorrow morning. Now I must apologize for not lingering. I want to get down that mountain road to Corona by daylight."

As I showed him out, I encountered Rosy in the hall. "I'm just going up to press her blue dress for tomorrow. She'll want to be wearing it," she said fondly.

That reminded me that I wanted to let Dorothea Mac know of Eugenia's passing. I didn't know her phone number so I called the vet clinic and asked them to give her the message, burial at 1 P.M. tomorrow. Andy, Rosy, I, and Hobo kept vigil during the night.

In the morning, Andy and his hired hand dug the grave. When it was finished, Andy lined it with fresh-cut spruce boughs and sweet-smelling ferns. Rosy and I bathed Eugenia, shocked by the frailty her clothing had concealed. We dressed her in her lovely blue dress and wrapped her in a freshly-laundered sheet that smelled of summer lavender. I had always thought of Eugenia as a woman of substantial size but the slender bundle on the bed belied my memory. I wondered for a moment the old wives' tale I had read was true—that passing of life diminished the corporeal mass it deserted.

While Rosy tidied the room, I gathered the papers spread out on the vanity and put them in Eugenia's little suitcase to hand over to her lawyer.

Rosy was leaving the room when she raised one more concern. "If we are going to have food for the people who attend, what shall it be and shouldn't I get started fixing it?"

"No," I said quickly and firmly." Let's just get ourselves ready to greet people at the veranda."

At 1 P.M. a small group had gathered in the parking lot: the Stevenses, Burr Worman, Dorothea Mac, and Ralph Hull, Eugenia's lawyer. Mrs. Mac came with an armload of brilliant pink and gold gladioli. Andy brought down Eugenia's body in his arms, and took the path to the cemetery, followed by Rosy, me, and Hobo as chief mourners, then the guests. Andy and Neil Stevens tenderly lowered the body into the grave, arranged the ferns and gladioli over it, and all of us joined in the Lord's Prayer. Andy read the Twenty-third Psalm, and I read the Beatitudes. Rosy sang in soft tones of crossing the troubled waters of life to the glory on the other side. After a few moments of silence at the graveside, Rosy led the guests back to the house. Hobo and I stayed while Andy and Neil filled the grave and replaced the sod cover. Back at the house, Rosy had furnished the guests with cold drinks and cookies on the veranda. We said our farewells, shook the guests' hands all around and watched them leave, except for Mr. Hull whom I invited to my office for a brief conference over Eugenia's papers. Hull asked Mr. van Houten to join us, since he and I participated in the terms of the will. I blessed the distraction; dealing with it relieved the poignancy of our mourning.

Mr. Hull opened the suitcase and the conversation with a compliment for the simplicity and reverence of the occasion. "I'm sure Mrs. Baker would have been gratified by the manner of her burial. As we wrote the terms of her will, she made it plain she wanted no 'parade' of a funeral. Her will provided only for a stone and engraving in the Bell cemetery."

"I'll see to that," Andy said.

Hull went on to outline the broad provisions of the will.

- Some 800 acres of land free of encumbrances to be signed over to the state with the proviso it be designated a wildlife refuge in perpetuity.
- Cash in the amount of $400,000 to establish an endowment for the maintenance of the property, with the proviso of a yearly salary of $5000 for Rebecca Bell as caretaker/manager of the refuge.

- Personal property to her dear friend Mrs. Rosenbaum for disposal however she might see fit.
- Andy named as executor.

I was dumfounded at the amount of cash Eugenia commanded. Although she had lived simply, I couldn't imagine how she could have accumulated that much money, even over a lifetime. I asked Mr. Hull if she had explained it to him. Timber sales over the years, he said, and hastened to add there were no taxes outstanding on property or income. He proposed taking the will to probate promptly. That reminded me that there were pots out on consignment at Country Crafts in Columbia. He said he would contact the store to redirect any income to the estate. Further he would provide a copy of the will to Andy and would be happy to answer any questions he or I might have.

Andy and I stood together on the veranda as Hull drove off. Andy had quite naturally put his arm around me. Now he said, "Do up the inscription for Eugenia's stone and I'll take it to the quarry man who did Mr. Willy's. Print two copies. We don't want any misspellings or misdatings. If it's OK with you, I'll specify the same size and finish as Mr. Willy's stone."

So I printed it out: EUGENIA MILLMAN BAKER, 1921-2011. Then I invited Andy to supper but he begged off, had cows to tend. I might have known.

With Eugenia gone, the days seemed very empty for Rosy and me. I began to worry that Rosy would start entertaining the idea of moving on. The two of us were working to put away the possessions still on the Baker homestead. Rosy decided to give the new wheel to the community college arts and crafts department as soon probate was complete. We stored away the tent, camp stove, and gardening tools in the Bell barn for later disposition. After we finished at the Baker homestead, all that remained was the superstructure of Eugenia's outdoor kiln and the ruins of the barn. Cassandra had reverted to her feral ways in her old territory although she occasionally paid a brief visit to Bald Knob to confront and hiss at Hobo. "She wants us to know she's gone but doesn't want to be forgotten," Rosy observed.

The day we cleared out Eugenia's room, I gathered my courage and blurted, "Rosy, what are your plans?"

She was turning and caressing Eugenia's needlepoint project in her hands. Although incomplete its pattern was well-defined. "I'm going to finish this. It will be beautiful. Eugenia had a real artist's eye and we had talked about the colors."

Impatiently I continued, "I mean, are you going to stay on here without her? Or will it be too boring for you with just me and Hobo and Sheba to look after?"

"What do you want me to do, Becca? Just say plain out! Don't just tell me to do whatever I *want* to do."

"I *want* you to stay. I'm like 'Enry 'Iggins, I've grown accustomed to your face. I would miss you terribly if you went away. Is that plain enough?"

"I want to be here as long as you want me here! How's that for a plain answer?" She dropped the needlework and threw her arms around me.

"I've grown to love you and leaving means I might have to drive down that godawful road to get away. Good reasons to stay, don't you think? Besides I'm happy here."

With my worries about losing Rosy put to rest, I got back to my translations and spent time with the family documents discovered in Cousin Willy's hidey hole. Although they were interesting, they gave up no major secrets. I missed Eugenia every day and Hobo and I started every walk with a visit to her grave site. The stone had been set up without a flaw in the inscription. My feelings were heartfelt but the visit was usually brief, Hobo was always in a hurry to get on with the walk. I found myself thinking about another something missing from my life. I hadn't settled things with Andy. The renovations in the house and Eugenia's death had occupied my mind to the exclusion of the memory of Andy's single passionate kiss. I turned my mind again to my relationship with Andy.

One morning I looked at myself carefully in the bathroom mirror and decided I had let myself go. I vowed to cream my weatherbeaten face, arms, and hands daily henceforth. My hair was rather shaggy, I would call Nell to get a trim. I resolved to dress up every day in the newer jeans and shirts. I cleaned, oiled, and polished my outdoor boots and made a note to walk with Hobo on dry paths. A week's worth of such minor repairs won me only one comment from Andy ("New shirt? Nice.") and convinced me that only a direct approach would end my indecision.

The opportunity came one evening when Andy came over as Hobo and I sat on the veranda enjoying the fresh spring breezes in the early twilight.

"If you aren't using your Jeep tomorrow, I think it's due for an oil change," he said.

The time is now, I thought. "Why don't you come up here and sit for while?"

We sat in companionable silence for a few minutes before I burst out, "What did you mean by kissing me on the mouth a while back?"

"Er, um, I'm sorry," he said, blushing fiery red and choking on his words. "I didn't mean to insult you."

"I wasn't insulted but I want to know why you kissed me that way. It seemed more than a casual gesture."

"I guess I yielded to impulse. I've wanted to ever since you appeared at Bald Knob that first day three years ago. But I've controlled myself although I have to admit that getting to know you better has made it harder and harder."

"Why has it been so necessary to bottle up your feelings? Can't you talk about them?"

"Damn it, Rebecca. All these months I've privately listed adjectives for you: beautiful, smart, compassionate, kind, caring, brave... a whole dictionary full. I can reel off the words and mean every one of them. But I don't think it's a good idea to tell you my feelings. You might understand them as love and love between you and me is out of the question from the get go."

"What in the world are you talking about?"

"Aren't you forgetting? You're heiress to a monumental fortune. I'm not a guy to play the princess and the pauper game. A significant relationship with you offers two options: a tawdry affair or marriage. The first is out of the question because you are too good for it and the second is out of the question because I'm not good enough for it."

I was getting more and more furious as I listened. I finally exploded. "If you've been smugly collecting adjectives for me, you should know I've spent a lot of time on a list for you. Not a bad point on it! Not good enough for me? Come off it! And how do you know I'm too good for an affair?"

"I'm flattered by your list. In spite of it, I'm just a cowman, manure on my boots, scratching out a living on a few hundred acres of rocks. It's taken me 10 years to get indoor plumbing in my cottage. You're the lady of the manor, in Mr. Willy's dream house, with every convenience. How do the two situations measure up, I ask you? And don't brag what a bad girl you could be. I'd be ashamed to offer you the chance! I sure don't understand your reasoning."

I flared up again, now my emotions were at the brim of tears. "Now you listen to me! I know what love is like. As a child, I loved my mother very much. I knew I belonged to her and she belonged to me. When she wasn't there any more, I knew I was alone. I had kind, affectionate, nurturing foster parents but I knew we didn't *belong* to one another. As I grew to be an adult, I came to realize that the kind of mutual belonging I hungered for would only come when I made a wholehearted commitment to a man who committed to me. I was alone and resigned to it. In time, I thought, I'd meet that man and have that mutual belonging that I needed."

I was so mad, I wasn't talking, I was spluttering, stumbling over the words that insisted on spilling out.

"Your kiss made me wonder if my dream might be coming true. Cousin Willy's crazy scheme brought me to Bald Knob, a place where I learned who I am, where I know I belong, and where I want to be until I join all those other Bells and Eugenia up there in the family cemetery. But as important as that is, I still haven't found that man, unless it's you. And you reject me because of some damn money I might get and definitely don't want. All I claim for a dowry is Hobo and Bald Knob. The ridiculous salary the estate pays me is going into investments just in case I'm still alone in my old age. It's beginning to look like that's how it will be—*alone in my old age, rich and unloved!*"

Andy burst into laughter so hearty and unexpected that Hobo jumped to his feet in alarm. Then realizing how silly my peroration sounded, I joined in the laughter. Andy put his arm around me and held me close until we had both achieved a degree of composure.

I was at last able to ask what was so funny. Andy snorted and replied, "*Unloved!* That's an adjective that never made it to my list. You can count on my love, Rebecca, now and forever. Just don't count on my investing it in a relationship that dishonors you or me. The stumbling block exists and I haven't the faintest notion how to get around or over it."

I thought I had an answer to my uncertainties. I threw my arms around Andy and put my face up to his, seeking his lips. I was rewarded by a fierce embrace and another passionate kiss. When we pulled apart, I was breathless, panting with an unfamiliar but very agreeable sensation. Andy cleared his throat loudly and his voice shook as he said, "I'll be over at six to work on the Jeep." And then he was jumping on his ATV and roaring off and away.

I stayed on the veranda my mind a jumble of serious thoughts until the crescent moon rose. Then I locked up the house and went to bed, Hobo close on my heels.

For the next few days, Andy and I studiously avoided one another—I, embarrassed for my brash behavior and he for his own reasons. Then a household crisis broke the deadlock. The connection of the water line to the powder room toilet came unstuck and neither I nor Rosy could get the valve to close. Facing a mini flood, in desperation Rosy called Andy. He came promptly from whatever he was doing in the meadow closest to the barn, and in no time, he had the line fixed and Rosy was plying him with freshly baked cinnamon buns. As I mopped up, I had formulated a verbal gambit to get back to talking about us with a minimum of embarrassment for him—and me! But I was too slow and he got away before I got my words arranged.

The next morning Hobo and I visited the cemetery. As I sat on the stone bench, with Hobo leaning close against my knee, I spoke to him, "What do you think Cousin Willy would expect me to do? You knew him better than I. I know he had come to believe I was a true Bell: bold, decisive, worthy of my lineage. What would he think of me if I "rared up" and flew in the face of his scheme to preserve Bald Knob and keep you with me as long as you lived?"

Hobo locked his gaze on my eyes and reacted to the tension in my voice with a soft woof. Then he got up and walked to Willy's grave. Pawing at the slight mound, he looked at me as if he were saying, "You're a Bell, do what is right for you!"

"Thank you. You got it right. Don't be afraid to be yourself. I know now what I'm going do. First I'm giving you a big hug, come here."

Hobo jumped up and danced over to me. We went back to the house and then Hobo and I got in my jeep, drove down Hudson Road to the Corona road, then up Barber Road. Andy's ATV was parked outside his cottage. Andy was in the little room he called his office shuffling papers. He looked up, surprise and alarm on his face, anxiety in his voice. "What's wrong on Bald Knob? Why couldn't you call? Is Rosy OK?"

"Everyone on Bald Knob is fine except me. There's a question I must ask you. If all I had in the world was Hobo and Bald Knob and a few thousand dollars in investments, would you take me seriously? I mean, then would you consider asking me to marry you?"

His expression turned into a mixture of amusement and dismay. "What's this all about? I'd consider asking you to marry me if you were barefoot and penniless. But you're not and no way are you ever likely to be. I thought I had made it clear where I stood the last time we talked."

"You did, abundantly. I just wanted you to say you still meant it."

He got up from his desk and put his arms around me, kissed me long and hard, until both of us were breathless. When I regained my composure, I turned around and ran out of the house, jumped in the car, and took the road to Columbia. Somewhere along the way I stopped and called BO&S, announcing an emergency and demanding an interview with Dan ASAP.

Tiffany met me at the door and promptly ushered me into the inner sanctum. His white-haired secretary jumped up and threw open the door to his office. Dan stood so hastily that the papers on his desk were thrown into disarray. "Tell me, are you OK? Is Hobo? Where is he?" he said.

"I left him in the car. I'm OK but in a terrible pickle. You've got to get me out of it! I'm in love!"

Dan laughed so loud and long that he had to pull his immaculate white handkerchief from his pocket and mop his face dry of tears before waving me into a chair by his desk. "In love! How can that be a pickle? I've been waiting for this. Andy's a fine man and you're a lucky lady to be in love with him. Mr. Bell would give his enthusiastic approval."

"Wait till you hear about it." I burst into tears. "He says he loves me but he won't marry me because of that damned legacy. Says he's too proud to play the pauper to a princess. What can you do about Cousin Willy's crazy arrangements? All I want out of life is Andy and Bald Knob and Hobo. I can't give up Bald Knob or Hobo but I can give up money in a New York minute. I want you to make it happen."

Dan sobered immediately. "I'm not a fairy godfather, able to wave a magic wand and make the problem go away. William Bell for all his foresight never considered that a man who wanted to marry you would find your billions unwelcome. Is Andy's position on this unalterable?"

"Oh, yes," I boohooed.

I spent the rest of the day waiting while Dan went over every detail of Willy's will and the trust documents. About 3 P.M. after my umpteenth cup of coffee and three trips to the car to visit with Hobo, Dan came to me as I sat unseeing in front of some inane TV show.

"I can't find any legal loophole in Mr. Willy's arrangements that would let you give up the monetary legacy before you have inherited it. Or that would void your contract with the trust while Hobo is still alive. I will have to consult both the trustees and some superlegal authority before I can give you any answer to your problem and even then, it may not be the answer you want. I suggest you go home and try to stay calm until I've done some more research. I'll try to work fast and I'll call you with word of the progress in the meantime."

Downcast but obedient, I started for home, reviewing Dan's words, but 15 miles down the road I turned around. I had called to mind Cousin Willy's ways of doing things. I had a hunch that when he ran into a snag in his plans, he didn't waffle around. He didn't *re*act to it, he gritted his teeth, and *acted*. Back in Columbia, I rushed up to the offices of BO&S and barged into Dan's office past Tiffany and Dan's secretary without ceremony.

Startled and alarmed, he leaped to his feet. Before he could speak, I did.

"I insist on talking to the trustees. Call them and set up a meeting, as soon as possible."

"But, but…"

"No buts. Let me know when it's arranged." I turned and walked out of the office and out of the building, a little shocked at my own temerity. Nevertheless, I intended to fight for myself.

On the road again, Hobo sitting erect and attentive in the passenger seat, I talked it out. He listened to every word, every now and then reaching to touch my arm gently with his paw. I rehearsed my adventures and vicissitudes at Bald Knob, the history of my origins that I had discovered there, the events that had matured me and taught me to know myself, the way I had taken Andy for granted for three years before love and commitment had become an issue. I wasn't the same aimless girl who took on the care of Bald Knob and a dog when I signed that contract with the trust in Dan O'Leary's office. I was Rebecca Bell, emphasis on *Bell*, and I was in love with Andreas van Houten and intending to marry him and bear his children. I wanted a future on Bald Knob and with Hobo at our side and bedamned to Cousin Willy's billions. Why hadn't I made that clear to myself and everybody else sooner!

Although I had called Rosy in the morning to tell her where I had gone, I hadn't told her why. She was waiting on the veranda as I drove up. "I've been so worried. Are you OK? Why did your business with Dan or Ben take so long? Are you hungry? I made your favorite broccoli and chicken casserole. It'll be ready in 20 minutes."

I reassured her at length, told her just enough to quench her curiosity, and half an hour later was eating a generous helping of casserole with relish. She still had a question. "Did you and Andy have a fight? He's been calling here all day, says he has to talk to you."

"I'll call him after dinner. I want to talk to him as well." My tone must have forbidden further conversation because Rosy grew very quiet and turned her attention to feeding Sheba and Hobo.

I asked Andy to meet me on the stone bench overlooking Willy's grave. The spring breeze was nippy enough that I had donned Cousin

Willy's sheepskin jacket, as much for courage as for warmth. Andy and I sat wordless for a few minutes before I blurted out a confession of the day's confrontation with Dan.

"I'm sorry I upset you so much," he said, reaching for my hand. His warm grasp was as comforting as a hug. "I've been thinking about how selfishly I expressed myself. I had a long wait before could tell you of my love, and every day I considered the million reasons why I couldn't. Your inheritance was always the snag. Mr. Willy wanted you to have it and I felt bound to honor his wishes as much as I've honored him. I knew there was no way for you to refuse his legacy. He made the link between the money and Bald Knob and Hobo unbreakable." His words stuck in his throat and his grasp tightened painfully on mine.

"I haven't told you everything yet. I've made up my mind to confront the trustees and insist that they help us break the link. There has to be a way. What I want out of life is you, Bald Knob, and Hobo, and I intend to fight for that. Dan hasn't called me back about a meeting yet but I'll keep you posted. For now, can't we just cuddle and kiss and think about being in one another's arms?"

The moon was high in the sky before we parted. Rosy was waiting up for me with hot cocoa and a direct inquiry. "Did you and Andy make up?" My answer, an emphatic "Yes, indeed," promptly erased the worry from her face and she said, "Well then, it's time for bed. Izzy and me never went to sleep before we made up our disagreement."

The next morning Hobo and I visited our favorite trails. I was furnished with my cell phone, a bottle of water in my holster, the binoculars, and the determination not to dwell on what Dan's reply to my demand might be. When the phone rang, Hobo was investigating a mouse hiding in a hollow tree stump. I was standing in a patch of white and purple violets under blossoming branches of dogwood, savoring Spring on Bald Knob. Dan's voice was stiffly formal as he informed me it would take two or three days before he could get the trustees lined up. I had an impression he wasn't particularly happy with me. By taking the bull by the horns, I had probably offended his *amour propre*; he had after all been the middle man in my dealings with the trust. I resolved then and there to be patient and not nag him. While I waited, I turned out all the linen closets, dusted every room, cooked as much as Rosy allowed, got back to my translations and Cousin Willy's journals, and walked and walked and walked until Hobo was reluctant to see me don my walking outfit.

Finally, on the fourth day, Dan's secretary called. "Mr. O'Leary has set up a meeting for you with the trustees of the Bell estate. It will be held here in the firm's conference room at 9 A.M. Wednesday next. The board expects Mr. van Houten to be present as well." The invitation was rather chilly but I was ready. I let Andy know time and date. Although he wasn't enthusiastic, he said he would be ready too.

I rousted out the most recent fashionable addition to my wardrobe, checked it for loose buttons and dangling threads, and inspected it for cat and dog hairs. It was a lightweight wool pants suit, a marvel of elegant tailoring, spring green and accessorized with a long-sleeved, pale yellow silk blouse. I wasn't exactly pleased with my shoes (scuffed) and purse (too dainty) but Crayola remedied the scuffs and I decided on a briefcase (not that I had any special papers to carry, but it looked businesslike). Andy appeared in a neat navy blue suit, complete with power tie and crisp pin-striped shirt, and a surprise. We had agreed he would drive. Instead of his pickup he pulled up a brand-new dark green Buick sedan to the veranda. To get to Bald Knob he had to drive Barber Road to the Corona road and then up Hudson Road. When I commented, he informed me, rather sharply, that as an official suitor of Rebecca Bell, it behooved him to appear to the trustees as a conservative businessman instead of a backwoods clodhopper.

Exactly at 9 A.M. Andy and I were ushered from Dan's office into the conference room. Off to one side a stenographer bent over a tape machine and a stenotype. On one side of the long, bare, highly polished table sat three unsmiling people: a white-haired beautifully coifed and dressed woman, a hulking man wearing an ill-fitting toupee, and a second man who needed only a bright red suit to play Santa Claus. There were no chairs on the other side of the table; Dan sat at one end of it and Ben sat at the other end behind a pile of ledgers and file folders. Andy and I were waved into position to stand opposite the three trustees.

The woman trustee made some opening remarks that established her as the chairperson. Then she said, "Young man, tell us something about yourself."

Andy cleared his throat and began, "My name is Andreas van Houten. I was born in the Netherlands but I am now a naturalized citizen of the U.S. I am in love with Rebecca Bell and aspire to have her for my wife and mother of my children. I can bring to the marriage an ethic of hard work and honesty, a four-room cottage, a few hundred acres of scrub land, a herd of cows worth about fifty thousand dollars, operating capital of another fifty thousand dollars plus a few thousand dollars in investments. The impediment at the moment to Rebecca's and my dream is the huge disparity between my net worth and her expectations."

"Thank you for your candor and compact communication. Rebecca, let us hear from you."

I gulped and tried to call to mind all the words I had rehearsed in preparing for this moment, but they poured out in a disorganized spate anyway.

"You should know that being Rebecca Bell is very important to me. When I signed the contract with the trust, I was a purposeless, feckless adult orphan. As caretaker of Bald Knob and Hobo, I have grown into a whole person. I have learned of my origins, I have made good friends, and I have learned to love Andy—er, Mr. van Houten. I am sure that William Bell intended with the contract he specified to guarantee that I would treasure and make every effort to preserve the heritage of the Bells on Bald Knob and furthermore, give his faithful companion, Hobo, loving care and a home as long as he lived."

I stopped long enough to catch my breath before continuing. WigMan yawned, but Santa and Madame Chair continued to pay close attention. I continued.

"I never thought ahead when I signed on that I would come to know and cherish the man with whom I want to share the rest of my life. Now all I want in my future is a life with Andy, our children, a home on Bald Knob, and Hobo at our side as long as he lives. I am told that there is no way I can avoid inheriting the vast fortune William Bell planned for me. With Hobo's death, I'll be stuck with it. Given that Hobo is likely to live at least ten more years, I will be in my forties and past my prime for bearing children before I have control of the contents of the trust. If I could control that inheritance this very day, I would turn it into the William Bell Foundation with a mission of granting engineering scholarships and development funds to innovative inventors. I would be free of all that damned money and Andy wouldn't have serious misgivings about marrying me."

WigMan, thoroughly awake, interrupted with a question. "What if Hobo dropped dead this very day?"

"I would be mortally sad. Hobo is my companion, friend, and confidant. I love him very much, and I want him alive to help me bring up our children. My next move would be to start the paper work for the William Bell Foundation. Since the contract would be void, I'd ask Andy if he would find my only dowry of the Bald Knob property and the few thousand dollars in my personal savings acceptable."

"What if Andy said it would?" Santa, with a twinkle in his eye, broke in.

"I'd be picking out a wedding dress."

WigMan and Santa burst out laughing. Madame Chairperson remained expressionless as she dismissed us. "You and Mr. van Houten may now leave us to our deliberations. Thank you for coming."

Andy and I joined hands and Dan rose and saw us out of the room.

Dan's secretary made us comfortable with coffee and snacks in the law library.

"What do we make of all that?" I asked Andy but he only shrugged and picked up a bread stick. I followed his example, I saw nothing else to do except read the spines of THE LAWS OF THE STATE OF INDIANA. While Andy browsed a couple of dog eared copies of *Field and Stream* he found on a shelf, I dozed.

At 12:45, Dan's entry woke me and Andy dropped his magazine with a start. Dan's face was carefully noncommittal. "The trust is offering you a deal. The trust is empowered to *sell* the Bald Knob property to Rebecca and to amend the contract. A revised contract will not provide the salary she has had or pay the expenses of the Bald Knob property as it has. That means Rebecca will have to pay for insurance, taxes, repairs, and such from personal funds. The revised contract will continue to require Rebecca to provide a home for Hobo as long as he lives. The proviso in Mr. Bell's will that gives her control of the contents of the trust when Hobo dies will stand."

I gasped in surprise, shock, and gratitude that I might be able own Bald Knob and keep Hobo. However, my heart sank when I saw the disappointment in Andy's face and he said, "I'm glad that the critical features of Mr. Willy's wishes for Rebecca and Hobo could be honored, but a deal would only delay her inheritance of the bulk of the estate. From what we know, the sale of the Bald Knob property would barely affect the huge size of the rest of the estate. Furthermore, how do we know she could afford what the trust will ask for Bald Knob?"

Dan hastened to address the last first. "As you know Ben Bender is thoroughly familiar with Rebecca's personal resources. The trust proposes a price between ten and one hundred dollars for the property. Ben assured us that the income from Rebecca's investments would more than cover the expenses of the property."

"Dan," I said. "Can't I take this deal for now and then sign something that binds me to live up to my intent to establish the William Bell Fund when I inherit the rest of the estate? Andy, my love for you makes me ready to do anything to make you trust me. If it takes a written, signed, and sealed document to make you trust my spoken word, maybe you don't love me as much as you've said. Maybe your pride is stronger than your love for me. Without trust maybe marriage isn't right for us and we should walk away from this right now. I'd live through it. I've lived through worse. But I'd never be happy again." Then my emotions got the better of me and I burst into tears.

Andy's face paled under his tan. "Good God, Rebecca, when you put it that way, I realize what a selfish egocentric ass I've been. Your vast fortune could never diminish my love for you. I'm ashamed to have driven you to question my devotion to you. Forgive me!"

Dan stood by amazed as Andy took me in his arms to rain kisses on my wet face while he murmured tender words of reassurance. Several minutes passed before Dan ventured a meek suggestion, "We can write up a prenuptial contract that would do the trick, if you two are willing." We turned to him like two sleepers waking to the morning sunshine. I told him to notify the trust that I was taking the deal. He left us with his congratulations and the promise to get right on the paper work.

Andy and I were very quiet as we traveled back to Bald Knob, only exchanging shy glances like two teenagers after their first kiss. We were conscious of a new beginning.

Rosy and Hobo, by some indescribable ESP, knew a good thing had occurred. Our arrival triggered Hobo into a frenzy of excitement, gamboling, barking, dancing on his hind legs. The moment we came in the door Rosy sent Andy to the cellar for wine. She had prepared a grand dinner: roast pork loin, garnished with Irish and sweet potatoes, flanked by baked apples, and followed by pecan pie. We honored her effort with hearty appetites exercised in the new dining room. Table conversation, fueled by liberal servings of wine, informed her of developments so far and the projections. She was so surprised and pleased that she almost forgot to eat.

"When's the wedding?" she asked.

"We'll have to take it slow, Dan and Ben have to do a lot of research and paper work. But maybe September. Fall is nice, colorful, not too hot, not too cold," I said.

Andy grimaced. "Maybe we can push them to an earlier date. I've waited a long time and I'm ready now."

Rosy and I rushed to explain. There was so much to do, we needed time for the preparations.

As it turned out, my suggestion for September worked out just right. In mid-August I had the deed to Bald Knob in my hand, I had signed an amended contract with the Bell Trust, and Andy and I had signed prenuptial agreements that Andy found acceptable. The wedding dress—knee-length cream-colored lace sheath—had been purchased and altered and hung in my closet. Satin shoes, dyed to match, their inch-and-a-half-inch heels requiring me to practice every day to learn to walk in them—if I never ever wore all the finery after the wedding, I would have no regrets. Andy and I, two tall people, would make a handsome picture standing together with Hobo in the big living room of Bald Knob on September 6 in front of our favorite friends, making our vows before a justice of the peace recruited from Greenwood—a picture and a day to remember forever.

Rosy was all in a dither; as my attendant she was to be garbed in brown satin. Bouquets of golden chrysanthemums were planned. When the day came, Hobo took everything in stride. In honor of the event he calmly and gracefully accepted a houseful of strangers.

That evening when everyone was gone and Rosy had gone to bed, Andy and I cuddled on the sofa in front of a dying fire, Hobo sprawled at our feet.

Suddenly, between kisses Andy asked, "Mrs. van Houten, will you let me live in your house? I brought over my pajamas and tooth brush this morning just in case you said yes."

"No question," I breathed.

As if agreeing, Hobo heaved a huge sigh of content and rolled over.